G.L.O@myspace.com

Co/Author

Capt of sales promotions

The Satisfier

NATHANIEL DALEY

Bloomington, IN

Milton Keynes, UK

AuthorHouse™
1663 Liberty Drive, Suite 200
Bloomington, IN 47403
www.authorhouse.com
Phone: 1-800-839-8640

AuthorHouse™ UK Ltd.
500 Avebury Boulevard
Central Milton Keynes, MK9 2BE
www.authorhouse.co.uk
Phone: 08001974150

First published by AuthorHouse 5/19/2006

ISBN: 1-4259-3904-X (sc)

Printed in the United States of America
Bloomington, Indiana

This book is printed on acid-free paper.

Chapter One

Marcus Smith and two of his closest friends grew up in the worst part of North Philadelphia. These guys had been as one since they were little boys playing in the sandbox. Living on the same block, they had been through a whole lot together. It was the year 1999 and tonight they were getting together to celebrate Marcus's twenty-first birthday.

Marcus was your average smooth-talking guy; he was so good with his words he could talk a girl right out of a coma. He was brown-skinned and had nicely done corn-rolls that he paid to get done every week. He stood about five feet and nine inches and was extremely built. Marcus had been seeing Ceria Williams since his freshmen days at Northern High School. She went to a different college than he was going to, and she thought it would be best if they went their separate ways. Ceria was Marcus's first love and he never did get over her. None of the girls he dated were as satisfying as his first love. Marcus figured that the strip club would be the best place to celebrate his birthday, and just maybe he could get his ex-girlfriend off his mind.

Brian Jackson, a.k.a. King, was the oldest out of the group. King was twenty-three. He lived with his aunt in North Philly. King's father left his family when he found out his wife was addicted to drugs; King was only five years old and couldn't understand why his father didn't want him or his mom anymore. King's mother later died from a drug overdose when he turned eleven, and his Aunt Helen took him in with her two daughters. Growing up in Philly young and black with no parents meant destruction. King did get in plenty of trouble as a youngster, but his two best friends would always be there for him.

All King's stories about the exotic clubs just made Marcus more anxious that he was turning twenty-one. King looked old for his age, so some of the older guys would take him to the local bars when they had a chance. King ended up not finish high school. He was to busy being the youngest pimp in Philly at the age of seventeen. He had a few girls working for him before he got arrested. After serving three years on probation, he decided that pimping wasn't for him.

Then you've got their homeboy Jamal Cornell, better know as Redd. King gave him that nickname back when they were in elementary school. He called him Redd because he was the only light-skinned boy on the block with reddish hair. Redd's father was Latino and his mother was African American. Redd had his father's features and his mother's nappy hair. He was twenty-two and he had a muscular build that drove the Spanish girls crazy; he was six foot and weighed 190 pounds of all muscles. Redd went off to play college football at Ohio State for a few years. He later dropped out when he discovered that he had a baby boy on the way.

A horn started blowing. Marcus could recognize that horn anywhere; it was King in his '87 Cadillac out in front off his house. This car was a piece of shit, but King still managed to pick up girls in it. This was the first car that he ever bought with his own money, and he loved that car to death. His Caddy was red with a torn-up leather interior and a terrible paint job on the outside. That's when Marcus came to the door and snapped at him.

"King stop blowing that loud-ass horn around here! You going to wake up my pops, and you know how he hate to be disturb!"

"Just hurry up and get in the car!" King retorted with authority.

Marcus got in the car wearing a pink Polo shirt and a pink, fitted Phillys hat.

"So where is the red-haired kid hiding out at. I been trying to reach his ass all day," Marcus said, referring to his friend Redd.

"Last I heard he was going to his babyma's house," King stated while turning on Broad Street. That's when Marcus's cell phone started to go off, and sure enough it was Redd. He never did miss a cue.

"So where you at?" Marcus asked Redd.

"Tell King to drive that hoopie over Layla's house to scoop me up. I just got off work and I had to take a quick shower."

They headed toward West Philly to pick up Redd when King popped a mix tape in the cassette player. Marcus listened to a few bars of the song and asked, "Who is this spitting so hard against these other industry rappers?" King told him that this was a new artist.

"This is Fifty Cent. I am telling you, Slick, that this cat is going to be huge one day." King turned the music up and started bumping, "How to rob an industry's nigga?"

Redd stayed with his father not too far from King's aunt's house in North Philly. Mr. Cornell worked hard at the boat's factory, but he had a bad drinking problem and he got very abusive toward his family. So Redd's mother divorced him and moved to Seattle. Redd's older sister, Reese, just got married and was living in LAN Chester. Redd stayed with his pop even though they stayed at each other necks. He felt that somebody had to look after him.

Redd had a two-year-old son by a Spanish girl from West Philly. After Layla Rivera had Redd's baby, she got really thick and she developed a nice-sized booty that made all the guy's heads turn to catch a second glimpse. Their relationships wasn't the same after he found out that she was cheating on him with a big-time drug dealer out of German Town who went by the name of Tony Allen, a.k.a. T-Bone. After T-Bone beat her ass a few times, she was begging Redd to take her back. Redd only took her back because he thought it was the best thing to do for little Jamal.

King pulled up to Layla's house and Redd was on the front porch waiting for them in a throwback Wilt Chamberlain jersey. They pulled up to the curb and he got in the car. He jumped in the back and said, "So what up, fellows?"

"Nothing much. You ready give these hoochies your dollars?" King asked Redd.

"If it wasn't Slick's birthday, I wouldn't be giving nobody shit. You know I don't got doe like that," Redd responded.

He and King started calling Marcus Slick back when he was a freshman in high school. Marcus would talk really slick and always had a way with words. King was the ladies man and Redd was the muscle of the crew.

King was seeing three different girls at one time. That's was the whole reason he called himself King. They loved his long, slim body. He was light-skinned with dark, wavy hair that drove girls crazy. He also went to Ill Will, his barber, every week just to get his hair cut and dyed dark black.

King had a Spanish mommy that he was going out with for about three years now. Marie was sexy with a body out of this world. Marie didn't speak English well but she could say King without any problems. Marie stayed in the hood on Girard Street on the other side of North Philly with her mom and little sister. King spent most of his time with her because she could dish up some rice and beans. Marie's head game was so extreme and intense that King got satisfied every time he spent with her. One thing that a man definitely loves is a girl who knows how to satisfied her man.

King's second chick lived somewhere in West Philly. King liked Denosh Lenox because she was Jamaican and she was loaded with money. Denosh's father was the biggest Jamaican's drug smuggler to come out of Philly. Pushing tons of Jamaican's gongja (exotic weed), Floyd Lenox made his daughter a hood princess by buying her anything her heart desired. Denosh drove around in a 2000 BMW, the 740 IL series. She bought King a Pasha 42 Cartier watch with an iced-out bezel that was worth thousands. Every king needed diamonds and that watch was ostentatious.

The third girl on King's list was Bethany. She lived in Camden County in a huge house in Turnersville. Beth worked in Philadelphia at Comcast's main tower as a computer technician supervisor. King liked her because she was an attractive white girl with a nice ass. She had great credit and it seemed as though she was going somewhere in life. King figured that he needed a girl on his team that had her head on straight. Every time she drove around in the hood looking for King, the females who lived in North Philly would be like "who is this chick." Beth wasn't your average white girl, though, because she would pull up into anybody's hood with nineteen-inch rims on her brand new

Jeep Wrangler, looking for her King. Even though all the girls hated on her, she could of care less.

They arrived at the strip club, *The Hole In The Wall.* The line stretched all way around the corner with young men waiting anxiously to see some ass get shaken. They parked and went right to the bouncer that King knew. Minutes later they were surrounded by girls with substantial ass and lumpish breasts. Exotic dancers swung around ten-foot poles while the other dancers gave out enticing lap dances. Marcus was having a blast and King wanted to do something even more special for his birthday.

King went up to this dark-skinned dancer that went by the name of Chocolate. He whispered softly in her ear.

"See that guy over there? Well tonight is his twenty-first birthday and I was wondering if you could take him in the back and do something really nice for him." She took a quick glance toward Marcus's direction.

"He is kind of cute, but that going to run you a hundred and fifty dollars. If he just want some head, that's going to be fifty," Chocolate responded very boldly. King pulled off a fifty-dollar bill from his stack and gave it to her. She went over to Marcus and put her hand on his shoulder. She pulled him closer toward her and whispered in his ear.

"That guy over there just paid for your birthday present. Let me show you what it is." Chocolate took him by his hand and directed him to the back of the club. She took him inside the champagne room and sat him down on the exotic couch.

Chocolate asked Marcus, "You like what you see, baby?" Marcus grabbed her by her apple-shaped behind as she shook it to the beat. She grinded on Marcus as he quickly got aroused. Chocolate grabbed him by the large bulge that was busting out his pants, and she was quite pleased about the size.

She instantly stopped dancing and took his well-equipped tool out of his pants; she bent down and put her tongue on the tip of his manliness. She proceeded to go all the way down and started giving him the most rigorous blowjob that he ever had in his life. Marcus, King, and Redd went home that night very satisfied.

Chapter Two

Marcus slammed his hand on the snooze button so the alarm clock would stop going off. Marcus was due at work in one hour. He took a quick shower and was going out the door right before his dad said, "Marcus make sure to get that trash before you leave."

He looked at the trash and than looked at his watch. He was already running late, so he decided he would do it when he got off work. Marcus worked in a small warehouse that was in Germantown. Lifting boxes weighting from sixty pounds to a hundred pounds for twelve hours a day could do wonders for the body. Even though his job gave him a great workout, Marcus made nine dollars an hour and had to work extra hours. Marcus wanted more in life.

Marcus came from a well-respected family, and they tried to raise their son with good morals. Marcus's pops worked at Temple University as a janitor, and his mom cleaned houses in Chester in the suburbs. Marcus's father resided in Philly all his life and met Marcus's mom when they were in high school. Marcus's mom was born in Atlantic City back in 1957. Her parents later move to Philly when she was ten and have been there ever since.

Marcus got to work about fifteen minutes late and his boss was all over him.

"Marcus, this is the fourth time you been late this month."

"I know, sir, but the buses was running late and it's was totally out of my control."

"Just make sure it doesn't happen again!" Marcus's boss said very seriously. Marcus had to catch two different buses to travel across town, and he was getting really fed up with his job's bullshit.

It was time for Marcus to punch out from a long day at work. He was on his way to catch one of his buses to head home. That's when he noticed this black Beemer with dark tint blowing the horn at him. The window rolled down just enough for him to see the driver's face. It was his homeboy King in Denosh's BMW. Marcus walked over to the Beemer and noticed King had his Spanish mommy in the car.

"Slick, get in. I'm about to take Marie home. Then I'll take you to the crib," King said to Marcus.

King didn't work, but his pocket stayed full of money. Even thought he wasn't putting girls on the strip anymore, he still was able to get anything from his ladies. He was driving Denosh's whip, and he had his other girl in the passenger seat. Marcus, on the other hand, had to work six days a week, twelve hours a day. He was paying rent at his parents' house and he had bills up the ass; he had just enough money to get an outfit at the end of the week. King had the latest closes, the newest sneaks, and a nice-ass watch that was surrounded with diamonds. Marcus envied him just a little bit because he was doing something right. King dropped Marie off, and the two of them drove off.

"Man, I am tired of this bullshit job and catching all these damn buses. You have all these girls buying you nice shit. You driving around in this nice car. What am I doing wrong?" Marcus complained to King.

"It's funny you said that because I was thinking the same thing. This car is fly and everything, but it's not mine. Don't worry because I'm working on something for the both of us."

King dropped Marcus at home and headed to West Philly. Marcus went in the house wondering what King had planned for them. He hoped that it could get him paid and that he wouldn't have to work anymore. He noticed his pops sitting down in his favorite chair, watching his favorite sitcom, "Amen."

"So what's up, Dad?" Marcus asked.

"What did I ask you to do before you left this house this morning, son?" Mr. Smith asked Marcus very calmly.

"I know I forgot to take out the trash but—"

"But nothing. When I ask you to do something, that's what I mean," Mr. Smith snapped at him.

"All right, Dad! I will take it out now!"

"It's too late. I already did it because, if I would have waited for your black ass, then it would've never got done." Marcus's dad was furious at him. Marcus stormed down to the basement and slammed the door.

"I am tired of this. I got to go to work to take shit and come home to take more shit. It times to get my own damn place!" Marcus thought to himself.

Chapter Three

Marcus was in the basement lifting weight, getting big, when Redd's name appeared on his cell phone.

"Where you been hiding at?" Marcus asked when he answered the phone.

"Working late hours and Layla wanting us to be the married type. I really ain't had time for anything else," Redd responded back to Marcus.

"It sound like she got you on lockdown, dog," Marcus said with a slight giggle.

"You heard from King today?" Redd asked, trying to change the subject.

"Yeah. He gave me a ride in Denosh's BMW not too long ago. But check this out. He had Marie in it, driving her ass all around the whole city," Marcus said it like he was kind of jealous.

"King better be careful because Denosh's dad is no joke. I heard he's the boss of the Shottas gang and they ready to kill for absolutely nothing," Redd said, being very serious. Redd and Marcus ended the conversation with that conclusion. King had to be more careful.

King blasted the music while driving back to West Philly, and as soon as he got on Denosh's street the haters started hating.

"Who the hell is this dude think he is?" one man asked another guy that was standing on the opposite side of the street.

"I don't know, but he can't be coming around here snatching up our chicks," the second man said back to his friend while watching King drive by. He parked the car in Denosh's driveway. She watched him pull up and she met him outside in a pink tank top and tiny pink shorts. Denosh lived by herself with her two-year-old son by some Jamaican who was deported for drug smuggling for her father last year.

Denosh grabbed her car keys and asked, "What took your ass so long, mon?" Denosh had this sexy-ass Caribbean accent that drove King crazy.

"I got up with my homie Marcus and I took him to handle a couple of things," King responded while grabbing her by her tiny waist. He apologized for taking so long and kissed her overpoweringly. King knew exactly what to do to make her acquit him for almost anything, and within minutes she forgave him. She told him to just call her next time to let her know that he was all right. They went in the house and King went right upstairs with Denosh right behind him.

"Make sure you be quiet. Samuel is sleeping boye," Denosh said with a sassy tone.

They enter Denosh's bedroom and got right to it. Denosh took off her tiny shorts as King watched with amazement. She was wearing no panties underneath those little tight shorts. King immediately got undressed and started caressing Denosh's body very gently. He kissed her on her neck feverishly, making her very hot and horny. Denosh let out a soft moan, and King ran his tongue down to her shoulder. He lifted up her tank top and sucked on her aroused nipples while his finger massaged her juicy insides.

Denosh couldn't take the persuasion any longer and made King quickly put on a condom. He introduced his hard-on to her wet pussy. As soon as Denosh felt his huge cock going in and out of her, she came within minutes and roared out, "King, King, I bloody love you monnn!"

Chapter Four

Two years later

King was waiting for Marcus to get off work in a brand new Cadillac Eldorado. Marcus's face nearly dropped when he seen King behind the wheel of a 2002 Cadillac sitting on twenty-inch rims. He walked over to him and got in the car.

"Damn, King, when did you get this and how could I get myself one!" Marcus asked with astonishment.

"Man I going to tell you a little secret. If you satisfy a woman in the bed completely, they will buy you whatever you want. I got Beth to cosign for this Caddy and got Denosh to buy these twenty inches Savanna's rims," King said in a nonchalant tone.

It was the summertime and the Greek Festival was going on all weekend. They headed to South Street to show off his new car. South Street was the place where everybody would be showing off their fly rides. Marcus wanted to go home and change out of his work clothes, but they were already on their way to South Street. That's when Power 99 started playing "Hard Knock Life" by Jay-z. King turned it up and the two of them banged their heads to the beat. He rolled down all his windows so everybody that was outside could see that he had really came up.

They turned on South Street and the traffic was from bumper to bumper. King love to draw attention and he was doing one hell of a job. They found a parking spot and parlayed on the hood of the car. King's Caddy was a chick magnet. As soon as they parked, two girls walked right up to them.

"Where you guys from?" one of the girls asked.

"We are from the north side. My name is King and that's my man Slick. What's yours sexy?"

"I am Renee and that's my girl Yahkira. Why do you call yourself King?" Renee asked quizzically. King told her that was a complicated story and she was welcome to hear it some day. Renee was all into King and he was all into her. Renee flirted with him for a few more minutes and they ended up exchanging phone numbers. King hated cell phones because he felt they were a tracking device, so he never got one. He gave her Marcus's cell phone number and told her he would call her sometime next week.

Yahkira was this pretty girl with a honeycomb complexion. She had these green-hazel eyes and a goddess's body that made guys think twice before talking to her. She didn't seem that interested in Marcus, as she stood their admiring King the entire time. King noticed that she kept looking at him, so he told them that they could all get to together for a double date. King felt he could change Yahkira's mind after she saw his boy, Slick, out of his work uniform.

The two girls walked off. Both turned around and waved bye to them. Renee asked Yahkira while they walked away, "So what's your thought about the other guy?"

"Who? The one that had the lumber jack's uniform on? I wanted to holla at that guy who called himself King, but your stanken ass got to him first," Yahkira said in a playful tone.

"You're just mad because he wanted me and not you," Renee responded proudly back to her friend. The two of them were just happy that they met a guy with a fly-ass car, even if one of them had to take his friend.

King called the girls on Saturday to see if they wanted to go to David's Buster for their double date. Renee gave King the directions to her house, and told him they would be ready about eight o'clock. King and Marcus got to Renee's house and both girls came out dressed to kill. They got in the back of the car and King drove off. King turned on Delaware Avenue and parked the Caddy at the boat's lot that was next door to David's Buster.

They went to the front entrance and security asked them for their IDs. King and Marcus pulled out their IDs, and they both waited to see how old the girls actually were. Both girls pulled out there IDs and gave them to one of the security guards. Marcus and King both were happy that they were over twenty-one. They looked at each other and thought the same thing. They were going to take them to the club afterward.

They went inside David's Buster, and it was crowed. King took a great risk for going in there with Renee on his arm. He didn't know who the hell was in there.

Chapter Five

Marcus didn't say much because he felt that both the girls were after his mentor, King. They laugh at his jokes and flirted with him when the other girl wasn't paying attention. Marcus even caught Yahkira on occasion and didn't say anything about it. After playing video games and getting to know the girls better, King was convinced that they were ready to go clubbing.

Delaware Avenue was surrounded with beautiful women and luxury cars throughout the night. They went to

Club Transit. It was only a couple of blocks away from David's Buster. They decided to walk, being that the traffic was outrageous. With the line stretching out to the parking lot, it took awhile to get in the club. By the time they got in, the girls were ready to get their party on.

Renee grabbed King and pulled him to the dance floor. She was half tipsy as she moved her body to the song. She started grinding her booty all over King when the DJ put on one of Luke's song. They danced through a few songs before the DJ finally slowed the club down with some soft R&B. He gently kissed her on her neck, making Renee want him even more. She turned around while moving to the beat and rubbed on King's leg very slowly. He wrapped his arms around her neck and pulled her closer to him. King slightly slid his tongue in her mouth, and she got wet on the spot. They started French kissing in the middle of the dance floor. Yahkira was watching her friend and got kind of jealous. That's when she got desperate. She went up to Marcus and said to herself, "He is kind of cute. Why not?"

Yahkira walked over to Marcus and asked him, "Would you like to dance?" Marcus told her he wasn't interested in dancing at the moment.

She frowned and asked, "What's the matter with you? You haven't said a word to me all day. You don't like me or something?"

"Well I didn't want to sound like I am hating or anything, but I thought you and Renee was competing for King," Marcus responded as slick as he always does.

"At first I did liked King, but after seeing how cool you really was, I had a change of heart."

Marcus couldn't figure out what changed her mind, but he wasn't going to let this opportunity slip away from him. Even though she was probably lying, they went to the dance floor anyway. Yahkira shook her rounded ass on Marcus for a few club bangers until a fight broke out. Marcus noticed King was right in the middle of it all. He ran toward the direction of the fight, and all he could hear was, "Fuck you, King! You ain't shit but a bloody dog! I am going to get one of my cousins to kick your fucking ass!" Denosh bawled at King. She had caught him with Renee's tongue deep down his throat.

Chapter Six

King was at his aunt's house in North Philly when he found his new Caddy's tires had been slashed and the paint had been keyed.

"I swear to God I am going to kill that crazy bitch!" King thought to himself. King got dressed and jumped in his '87 Caddy, which was parked in the back of his aunt's garage, and headed to West Philly. King was fed up with Denosh's drama, and he was going to tell her to leave him the fuck alone. King parked his car in front of her house and went to bang on her door. Denosh came to the door and saw King with a face that told her he was ready to kill her. That's when she simply asked, "What do you want boye?"

"I swear to God, Denosh! If you don't leave my car the fuck of alone, I am going to get somebody to beat the piss out of you! I don't give two shits who your father is. Just leave me the fuck alone!" King replied while walking back toward his car.

"All I got to say is watch your fucking back, King!" Denosh retorted while slamming her door.

King went to his aunt's house and immediately got his new Caddy repaired. He took it over to Beth's house so some Jamaicans couldn't tried to wreck it again. After handling some business with Beth, he went to Girard Street and went to pay Marie a visit. She always knew how to relieve King's stress.

Denosh told her cousin, who was a high-ranked soldier of the Shottas gang, what had happened. When Floyd Lenox got the message that a street punk had disrespected him and his daughter, he went crazy. Devon told his uncle that he would handle such a small thing. One thing Mr. Lenox didn't like was a young punk fucking his daughter over, so he told Devon to make sure that he made an example out of him. He wanted everybody in the entire city to know that the Shottas weren't to be fucked with—or his daughter. Devon told his uncle that this pussy hole would never disrespect anybody ever again.

Devon got a photo of King from Denosh, and she also gave him King's aunt's address as well. Denosh's cousin meant business, and this was another chance to shown his uncle that he should be a leader in the gang. Devon and another Rasta staked out King's aunt's house for a few weeks, and there was no sign of King anywhere. Devon got the word that King was staying on the other side of North Philly.

The rumor in the hood began. "The Shotta's gang is looking for King." The word got back to him and he knew that he had to do something fast. He also knew that there was going to be all types of Jamaicans coming after him. King decided he needed a gun for some protection, and finding a gun in North Philly was like finding a wine bottle on the ground. You could find one on any block of Philadelphia.

So King went around searching for a gun. That's when he ran across Kenny. Kenny was a big-time drug dealer back in the day, and he even gave King a job as a lookout guy for his corner when King was only sixteen. After being locked up for so long, he didn't realize that the lookout guy had become a king. King was with two girls now and was driving around in two different types of Cadillacs. He didn't had to sell drugs or be anybody's lookout boy. Kenny got locked up for selling narcotics years ago, and he had gotten released about a month ago. King hadn't seen him since the day the cops threw the cuffs on him.

"So what's up, Brian? You still on the block?" Kenny asked while serving a customer.

"No, man. After you got locked up, I had stop selling drugs to our people," King responded politically.

Kenny noticed that his watch was full of real diamonds and he was wearing the latest gear on the market.

"You got to be in something with a watch like that," Kenny said while taking another look at his Cartier watch.

"I am a pimp now. I got girls buying me shit, but that's not important right now. I need a fucking gun," King said, confident that Kenny could help him out. Kenny had a man who was into selling guns and told him that he could get him one really cheap.

Meanwhile Marcus was getting more involved with Yahkira. After the ordeal at Club Transit, they figured that they would go on their own date together. They had ended up exchanging phone numbers and been on quite a few dates since then. Renee tried to convince Yahkira that Marcus was nothing but a dog like his friend, King.

"Birds of a feather flock together," Renee constantly reminded her. Yahkira insisted that Marcus didn't seem like that type and that he treated her really sweetly, so she continued to see him.

Marcus didn't have a car, and Yahkira would borrow her mom's car whenever they would go out. She started falling in love with Marcus because he was extravagant to the point that she felt like a queen. He would open doors for her, and every time they went out, he brought her the most dazzling flowers he could find. Yahkira had her share of assholes, and whoever treated her that sweetly deserved a chance.

Chapter Seven

Several months later

King stayed at Marie's house while her mom and sister went to Puerto Rico to visit her family. He told Marie he would be right back while he walked to the corner store to get a dutch. He wanted to roll up a healthy blunt after blowing Marie's back out. He needed something to relax his nerves. The store was right around the block, so he left his '87 Caddy in front of Marie's house. Devon, who was sitting in the passenger side of an Escalade truck, noticed King going inside the store.

"Oh rube boye, is that who I think is, mon?" Devon asked the driver. He looked at the picture that his cousin gave him, and he was now certain that was his target. After spending half a year looking for King, he had finally found him.

The driver did a u-turn and parked a few cars away from the store. King came out and headed back to Marie's house while rolling his blunt. Devon got out of the truck with his brethren who was doing the driving. They walked over to approach King. That's when Devon yelled out, "Rube boye! What's this bloody bullshit, that's you said, fuck da Shottas, mon? Mr. Floyd Lenox send his regards, boye." And the other Rasta chased after him with a big-ass blade and tried to end King's life right there. King instantly dropped the blunt and pulled out his Tec-Nine handgun that he had gotten from Kenny's man. Without hesitating, he pulled the trigger about four times. He hit the Jamaican that came after him with the blade once in the throat. Devon never had a chance to take out his gun, catching one of King's bullets right in chest and dying instantly.

One man witnessed the entire thing as King took off running, tucking the gun in his waist. He sprinted all the way to Marie's house, with people watching and wondering who was this man was and why was he so paranoid. They observed him while he rushed to get in the house. Breathing heavily, he ran in the house and locked the door behind him. Marie observed him and said to herself, "What the hell is going on?" He went through the back, up the alley, and stashed the gun behind some bushes. King went back in the house and explained to Marie what just happened.

Minutes later the police were on the scene and started investigating the shooting. An unidentified man was dead and a second man was in critical condition. The police questioned the man who had seen the entire thing. Still in shock, he explained what he saw. He told the police exactly what direction the man ran. The police traced King's tracks, and with a little help, they were knocking on Marie's front door. King knew that it wasn't worth running and told Marie to opened up the door and let them in. They searched the entire house for the murder weapon.

They brought King back to the site where the murder took place. Devon was covered up with a white sheet and the other guy was on his way to Temple Hospital. The witness told the police that King was the man that he had seen doing the shooting. They told him he had to testify to what he saw.

Yahkira was on her way to pick Marcus up when Redd called him on his parents' house phone. Marcus's mother yelled down into the basement that Jamal was on the phone.

"What's up, Redd?" Marcus asked while getting ready for his date.

"Turn to channel six right now!" Redd said with anxiety. He was very worked up. Marcus ran to the TV to see why Redd was so hyper. Marcus's mouth nearly dropped when he saw his friend's face all over the news.

Action News had a special report about a shooting in North Philly. The reporter stated what he knew.

"I am here live, as multiple gun shots took place on Girard Street. One local man is dead and another man is critically wounded. Brian Jackson, known in the streets as King, is believed to be the gunman in the shooting that occurred early today. Police had him in custody and were holding him in the county jail. Stay tuned until we learn more about this incident."

Marcus couldn't believe this. He was in complete shock. He rushed back to the phone to see if Redd was still there.

"Redd, are you still there?" Marcus said while trying to keep his cool. Redd responded back and told Marcus what he knew.

"I heard he killed Denosh's cousin in self-defense."

Marcus didn't know that the Denosh's incident had escaladed this far. Marcus asked Redd how he found out about all this. He told him that the streets got the information before any cop on the force did. Marcus didn't even know King had a gun. He later called Yahkira up and told her he had to cancel their date for tonight.

Chapter Eight

The next morning, Marcus stayed by the phone and waited for King to call him collect. Redd got to Marcus's house really early to see what he could do to help. They got the call about eleven.

"Slick, is that you? I need your help man," King said while sounding demoralized.

"Don't say no more. Just tell me what you want me to do," Marcus responded.

They gave King a million-dollar bail, and he knew that Beth's house wouldn't be enough for collateral. King heard about a Jewish lawyer who was supposed to be really good. King trusted that Beth was going to put up her house for his bail, but he just needed a bail reduction to happen first. If they cut his bail in half, he will be released really soon. That's where the Jewish lawyer came in.

"I need you to go over Marie's house and pick up some money and my old Caddy for me. Marie doesn't have a phone in her house, so I can't call her. Take the money over to Chester and find me a lawyer by the name of Jerry McGinnis. He could set me up for a bail hearing. They hit me with a million-dollar bail."

Marcus gave Redd Beth's phone number and told him to tell her to find the deed to the house. Beth was King's money train, and she did anything for her King. She had King's new Caddy parked outside while she drove around in her Jeep Wrangler.

Marcus stayed on Montgomery Avenue, and it was at least ten blocks away from Marie's house. Marcus jumped in a freelance cab and headed to Girard Street. He got out of the cab and saw four men standing out front of Marie's house. Two of them had dreadlocks, while the other two had on red, green, and yellow bandannas that read "Shottas" on them. Marcus was terrified and hoped that they didn't knew who he was. He walked right by the house as the men observed him like a hawk. He turned the corner and sprinted to the alleyway. Marcus had no choice but to leave the Caddy there. His life was in jeopardy if he didn't do so.

All the lights in Marie's house were turned off, and Marcus feared the worst. He got to the back of the house and went to the back door. He checked to see if it was possibly left unlocked. He turned the knob, and it was locked. He noticed a side window and tried his luck. Amazingly it was left unlocked! He opened it just enough so he could climb in. He called out Marie's name very quietly.

"Marie, Marie."

Marcus started to panic, thinking that he might be too late. The Shottas probably got to her and the money. He went to the bedroom and continued to call out her name.

"Marie, Marie." That's when he heard a voice. He checked the closet and found her. Marie's body was white, as though she seen a ghost. She was scared to death, and that's when she noticed who Marcus actually was. She got up and gave him a hug. She was relieved he found her and not those guys who was standing outside. Marie told him that those guys been out there all day. She showed Marcus where King kept his money and handed him a sneaker box. Marcus opened it up and the box was full of cash. Marcus thought to himself, "What is King involved in, he got all this money but don't have no phone in this house."

That moment Marcus knew that Marie couldn't stay in that house for another minute. Marcus dialed up Redd on his cell phone to see if he had gotten in touch with Beth.

"So what did Beth say to you?" Marcus quickly asked Redd.

"Beth told me she's looking for the paperwork to her house as we speak," Redd explained.

"Well, check this out! I got about four Shottas standing out front of Marie's house. I don't know what they are planning but I am going to take Marie out of here." Marcus and Marie packed up some of her belongings and a few things of King's, and they went out the back door and up the alley.

Chapter Nine

Marcus took Marie and put her in a motel. Marcus paid for two weeks' worth of the rent for her. He went home and went down to the basement. He opened up the sneaker box. He began to count King's money. After counting to twenty thousand dollars in cash, he looked in the yellow phone book and looked up Jerry McGinnis.

The lawyer set up King a bail reduction hearing for next week and charged Marcus two grand for the hearing. Jerry told Marcus, if Brian wanted him to represent him in this murder case, it would cost him fifty thousand dollars total. Marcus did like King asked and gave him nineteen thousand and five hundred dollars up front. He took out $500 for the motel that he paid for Marie.

Marcus's cell phone rang and it was Yahkira. She hasn't heard from Marcus in a few days and started to worry that he got caught up in King's beef. Marcus explained to her that he was all right.

"I am okay. I just been doing a lot of running around, taking care of some business."

"Damn, you could've called and told me you was all right," Yahkira snapped at Marcus as though they were married. Marcus responded back really slick.

"After I get finish with what I am doing, I promise you I will call you and we could go do something special for tonight." Marcus ended the conversation on that note, and Yahkira was happy.

Brian Jackson's bail reduction hearing was being held early in the morning. Marcus, Beth, and King's aunt were all in the courtroom. Redd couldn't make it because he had to watch his son. King walked in the courtroom wearing all orange, cuffs, and shackles on his ankles.

The district attorney was this white lady with a face that showed she meant serious business. She had her hair back in a ponytail; she wore her glasses on the tip of her nose. Marcus took one look at her and just knew that they weren't going to reduce King's bail. The prosecutor stated her case to the judge.

"Brian Jackson on Girard Street where a young man was brutally murdered. The second man is still in the hospital listed in critical condition. We have an eye witness who will testify that he was the shooter. No way this man's bail should be reduced. He will skip out on trail! Mr. Jackson is a flight risk!"

King's attorney, Jerry McGinnis, told the judge his client was innocent of all charges.

"Brian Jackson acted in self-defense. Knowing that his life was in danger, with an eight-inch knife drawn to his throat. He was able to defend himself just in enough time before these ruthless gang members were able to stab him. He will forfeit his passport. Brain just wants a fair chance to prove his innocence."

The judge listened to both attorneys and deliberated for a few minutes before reading his decision.

"Well, the state does have a strong case against Brian Jackson, being that a blade was found on the victim and no weapon was found on the suspect. I'm going to reduce his bail from a million dollars to five hundred thousand dollars." Brian's lawyer had told the court that Brian protected himself without actually telling them he was the shooter.

Marcus and Beth instantly got up and went to the court's clerk and put her house up for King's bail. After a few hours, King was released.

Chapter Ten

Soon as King made bail, he went right up to his aunt and gave her a hug. He then proceeded give Beth a kiss and whisper in her ear, "Beth, baby, I owe you so much." He looked over to Marcus and said, "And if it wasn't for you I will still be sitting in that hellhole." King was very blessed to be surrounded with the friends that he had, and he knew that this was only the beginning; the worst was soon to come. He had to get himself acquitted of these accusations.

King told Marcus he would be over to his house to pick up his things later. Beth and King dropped Marcus home and they headed to Turnersville. They got to Beth's house, and King saw that his new Caddy was untouched. They entered the house kissing like they hadn't seen each other in years. He closed the door behind them, and Beth quickly undid his belt buckle. King caressed her neck and her ear with his tongue, making her want him right there. He knew exactly where her weak spots were, so she immediately got moist and wanted to fill him the inside of her. She took off her Old Navy jeans and slowly pulled off her see-through thong. She stood there half naked as King admired her sexy body.

Beth turned around and put both her hands on the front of the door. King took out his hammer and started smashing it from behind. After Beth got weak in the knees and could hardly stand anymore, she told King to lie on the floor. She climbed on top of him and rode him, like there was no tomorrow.

After relaxing with a blunt, Beth had work to do. She was going to prepare a Web site for ladies at her job. King was having sex with the women at her job. That's how they were getting paid. She brought home a good paycheck every week, but what King brought in for his experience of what she just encountered was much more rewarding. Beyond a doubt, as an escort he was truly a satisfier.

King caught the bus to see Jerry McGinnis in Chester; he knew that the Shottas were probably still looking for him. So he decided not to drive his new Caddy—to play if safe. After signing all types of paperwork, King found himself on Girard Avenue at Marie's house. Marie's mom came to the door and told him she didn't know where her daughter was. She got really worried when she saw that she wasn't with him. He couldn't stop thinking what if Floyd Lenox had something to do with her disappearance. He went around to the alleyway where he stashed the gun. King looked through the bushes and was shocked that it was still there. He tucked it away in his jeans and went back inside Marie's house. He went through the back door and gathered the rest of his things. King told her mom that, when he found Marie, he was going to bring her home. He got in his '87 Caddy and headed to other side of North Philly.

King went to his Aunt's house and she was really happy to see him out of shackles. He gave her a hug and told her that it wasn't his fault.

"Aunt Helen, Denosh's cousin and his friend tried to stab me, and I had to protect myself." She just couldn't figure where she went wrong. She thought to herself, "Even though he was in trouble with the law when he was younger, a killer he definitely wasn't." King gave her another hug and told her he had some business to handle. He told her not to worry herself—that he would be back shortly. She told him to just be careful in those dangerous streets.

King jumped in his old Caddy and headed to Marcus's house. Redd and Marcus waited anxiously as King walked down the basement's stairs. King sat down and explained what really happened.

"I know that my case don't look good, fellows. They claimed that I murdered Denosh's cousin, but they tried to run down on me with a big-ass blade. It just so happened I bought me a gun and they ran down on the wrong dude."

That's when Marcus tried to tell him about the Jamaicans that were standing out front of Marie's house.

"Oh shit, Marie! I put her in a motel and totally forgot about her." They rushed over to the motel that Marcus put her in last week, hoping that nothing bad had happened to her. Marcus explained the whole story about the Shottas and how he gave Marie five hundred dollars to pay for the motel. King was relieved to hear that.

King knocked on the door and nobody answered. He knocked again and the door open very slowly. Marie saw King at the door and started crying.

"Hey, Papa, I miss you so much!" Marie was so happy to see him; she thought that this was a dream. King ran back to the car and told them he'd holla at them in a little bit; he had to take care of Marie really fast.

King walked in the room and Marie was already waiting for him, nude. The light was sparkling off Marie's tan complexion. He ran his fingers through her jet black, wavy hair that went all the way down her back. Marie just knew that this moment was never going to happen ever again.

King grabbed her by her thin waist and gently laid her on the bed. She kissed him on his neck and glided her tongue all the way down to his chest. He already knew where she was targeting, and before he could say another word, his eyes were in the back of his head. Marie did what she was most likable for, and King got fully aroused. She than crawled on top of him and conveyed him until she felt her juices ruptured all over King's stomach. Once again Marie was completely satisfied.

Chapter Eleven

Marcus and Redd were driving with no clue where they were going. Marcus just couldn't stop thinking about where King got twenty grand and how he already had sex with two different girls before they could even talk to theirs. Marcus looked at Redd and said, "Redd, what do you think King is involved in? I never seen him with any type of drugs except for the weed he smoke every now and then. I just hope he didn't hook up with that fool Kenny again."

"I don't know what he is into. But whatever it is, it's something huge," Redd responded.

An hour went by and Marcus's cell phone went up. It was King calling from the motel. He told Marcus to come and get him. Marcus did a u-turn and headed back to the motel. King got in the back as Marcus pulled off. Marcus gritted his teeth, wanting to ask King so many questions. "Where did the money come from? Where was his 2002 Caddy with the twenty-inch rims that got him in all this trouble in the first place?" Marcus thought. Marcus looked in the rearview mirror at King and noticed that he was just as calm as he could be. It wasn't like his life was in jeopardy or anything; Marcus just wanted to know his next move.

But most importantly, where in the hell they were driving to?

Marcus kept driving until he saw a Popeye's Chicken and pulled in. King sat in the back in complete silence. They ordered something to eat and ate their food in the car while they waited for King to give out his next move. That's when Marcus asked King, "So what now? You already know that the lawyer needs thirty thousand dollars more before he could represent you."

Marcus asked King how he was going to get the rest of the money without actually asking him. Marcus hadn't been to work for a few days and didn't know if he still had a job. He was more interested in how King got his hands on twenty grand than going to lift some frozen meat in a warehouse.

Marcus didn't know if King was going to beat his case or not, but he did know he wanted to live how King was living. He was just waiting for King to show him how to do so.

Redd, on the other hand, started to miss his family. He was quiet and didn't what to tell his friends he wanted to go home to his family. He really didn't know how much time he had left to hang out with King.

Chapter Twelve

Redd finally went home late that night and spent it with Layla. She was relieved that Redd was all right. Then she hit him on his arm and said, "Why you had me up all night worried about your ass? Better yet, why didn't you call me and tell me you were okay?"

"I am sorry, baby. I know I should have called, but I just got caught up with the fellows and lost track of the time. King could be going to jail for the rest of his life."

"Well, I know that the man that King oppose to kill. People are probably looking for him right now! I just don't want you to get caught up in the middle of it all. You got to start thinking about your family, Jamal," Layla said while caressing Redd's hands. He knew that she was probably right, but he also knew that King would do the same for him if the shoe were on the other foot.

Redd and Layla went upstairs and they quietly walked by her mom's door. They didn't want to wake her or their son. They went inside her room and turned off the night. Layla undressed her man in the dark. She massaged him very gently as he tried to get his best friend's murder trail off his mind. He turned himself around and pulled her toward him. He kissed on her neck and slowly brought down her nightgown.

Layla immediately got on top him and guided his cock inside her. She went all the way down and backed up very slowly while Redd caressed her perky tits. She got off him and wanted him to hit it from the back. Redd grabbed her from behind with both hands to give himself leverage. Smack, smack was the sound that went through her room. After about five minutes, Layla couldn't take the pounding anymore, but she insisted that he didn't stop. She finally came and her body collapsed on the bed.

Marcus and King headed to Beth's house late that night. They got on the Ben Franklin bridge and headed to Turnersville. King turned down the music and asked Marcus, "Did you ever think about where did I get twenty thousand dollars from?"

Marcus looked at him and said, "What do you think?"

"All right. Beth got these ladies that work at her job. Some of them are married, some are divorced, and some just want to be satisfied correctly. So Beth will set up the whole thing and I will charge them from anywhere to twenty-five hundred to five grand a night." What King had to say made Marcus very interested and want more details.

"Why didn't you tell me this sooner? I am down with something like that! So it's like you are a male escort?" Marcus asked.

"I like to call me the satisfier! Women pay me good money to satisfy them," King said very proudly. He convinced Marcus that this was the perfect opportunity that he was waiting for.

They got to Beth's house and Marcus noticed that King's new Caddy was parked out front. King looked at Marcus and grinned.

"This Caddy is now yours, and I'll let Beth know that you are ready to join the team."

"King, before you go, I wanted to ask you about Beth? What do she think about you banging other girls?" Marcus asked while wondering how he pulled this all off.

"At first she didn't want to go through with it, but after she seen all that money I made and then coming home to fucked the shit out of her, she was totally convinced."

King gave Marcus a pound with his fist and he was back on the road. He pick up his cell phone and dialed Yahkira's number on speed dial.

"Hello," Yahkira answered, sounding still asleep.

"It's Marcus."

"Boy, do you know what time it is?" Yahkira asked sternly.

"I just wanted to hear your voice." Marcus was a slick-talking dude, because he had Yahkira's full attention after he said that. She was kind of shocked that he call her so late. They talked on the phone until Marcus got back to Philly.

Chapter Thirteen

The next week Beth already had clientele set up for Marcus. Beth's company was consisted of fifteen floors and was mostly run by successful women. Beth had a Web page strictly designed for these ladies who weren't getting any at home or just weren't getting satisfied completely. Beth had King's and Slick's half-naked bodies posted on this particular Web site. The ladies were setting up appointments left and right, all wanting to be pleased in bed.

King had his own clients that couldn't get enough of him. A few times the ladies would asked Beth to join them, if the price was right. Then they had themselves an incredible ménage a trois, making these ladies fantasies thoroughly come true. Beth advertised at work "how Slick could do this" and "how Slick could do that." These ladies wanted to know firsthand how a multiple organisms felt.

Marcus wanted to do something a little different than his mentor. He wanted to set up a date first, before satisfying anybody. He did this just in case they were so vague that he wouldn't get into it and developed a bad reputation. He would set the dates at gourmet restaurants all throughout Philly.

With Beth doing all the arrangement, Marcus was waiting anxiously for his first client to meet him at a restaurant. That's when a middle-aged white woman wearing dark Chanel glasses sat down at his table. She introduced herself.

"Hi, my name is Mary. Beth told me that you wanted to meet me first before you do anything. I saw your picture on the Web page and I knew that you would be just right for me."

Mary was married and her husband was on the road a lot for business. She tried all types of male escorts, but none of them was fulfilling enough. She opened up to Marcus even more as they sat there and ate their food. They had a few drinks as Mary ran her eyes up and down his body, letting him know that she was ready to be taken care of.

Marcus told her that it was going to run her one thousand dollars. Since this was his first time, he didn't what to charge her like King would of charge her. They went down the street to a hotel that was nearby, and Marcus told her to freshen up and he was going to get some wine to make this evening a little more special. Mary liked something about him and couldn't figure out what it was.

When Marcus returned, he had brought some roses for her. He poured some wine in a glass and Mary was amazed how smooth he actually was. Mary only wore a towel to cover her naked body, and Marcus took off his Polo shirt, revealing how built he really was. Then he took out some candy-favored oil. He told her to lay down keeping the towel underneath her so the bed wouldn't get any oil on it. He poured it very gently on her left foot, sucked on her smallest toe first, and worked his way up to her big toe. When Mary felt the sensation of Marcus's warm mouth, she starting moaning, letting him know that he was doing it right. He thought to himself, “Shit a thousand dollars was on the line. I had no choice but to do it right.”

Marcus poured some more oil on her breasts and suck on her nipples while he was playing with her moist insides. He put some more oil on her warm, wet, and ready-to-be-fulfilled pussy. He started on the citrus and Mary climaxed immediately as she felt his tongue with the combination of hot oil rapidly going in and out of her. Mary’s body left and went to paradise. Before Marcus realized it, her juices were erupted all over his face. He didn’t stop, though. He held his breath and continued to suck on her. Mary wrapped her legs around Marcus’s head and yelled out, “Oh my lord, I am, I am coming againnn!”

Chapter Fourteen

Marcus made his way to Beth's house to tell King the high quality job he had done. He gave King five hundred dollars to put away for his case. King within two weeks already made eighteen thousand dollars. He wasn't playing around. He knew that he was facing life in prison and he needed to pay this Jewish lawyer if he was going to have any chance of beating this murder's case. Some of King's clients knew that he was looking at some serious indictments but that just turned them on even more. They loved him and what he was capable of doing in bed.

"So how was it?" King asked Marcus.

"Man, that was the most easiest money I had ever made in my life. A thousand dollars for just eating some pussy. I am hooked," Marcus responded while counting the rest of his money.

Beth went to work the following morning and the word was in. "The man who calls himself Slick makes you cum multiple times without using his dick," Mary told her coworkers, and they told their coworkers. Beth's Web page was buzzing with horny ladies all wanting what Mary experienced.

Mary was so please with Marcus's work she told her younger sister who had just gotten recently married. Marsha's husband was terrible in bed, but he was a wonderful father. Mary gossiped about Marcus spectacular tongue's action and gave her the information on how to get in contact with him. Marcus was slick and he knew that Mary was going to want more, so he gave her his cell phone number. That way he could cut out the middleman and didn't have to pay Beth for her services.

Meanwhile Marcus's clientele was increasing. More women wanted to be satisfied and Marcus was meeting their expectations. The money was rolling in, but he decided to keep a low profile. He went to the Gallery and bought a few new outfits and some nice dress shoes. Marcus was taking this opportunity like a real career.

After shopping, he called up Yahkira and told her that they were going out tonight. He drove his '87 Caddy to her house, and Yahkira came out looking like she was a version of one of the girls off Top Model. Marcus almost forgot how attractive she truly was. She wore a tennis skirt with a tight Gucci shirt that made her breasts look bigger than they actually were. She got in the car and gave Marcus a hug.

"So where do you think you're taking me tonight?" Yahkira asked while smiling the entire time.

"I wanted to take you somewhere special," Marcus said while headed to Lincoln Drive. Yahkira didn't care where he took her. Yahkira was just happy that Marcus was spending time with her. She had dated nothing but assholes only wanting one thing from her. The entire time Marcus was with her, he had never pressured her to have sex, and that turned Yahkira on more than anything.

Yahkira rested her hand on Marcus's knee as he drove downtown; he turned onto Broad Street while playing some old R. Kelly. He then pulled in a parking lot that Yahkira wasn't familiar with, and she asked, "Where are we?"

"Have you ever heard of Def Jam Poetry? Well tonight they are airing their show right here at the Arts Bank café, and it's starring Mos Def."

They went inside and sat at an empty table. The café was crowed with other couples waiting for the first poet to hit the stage. The show was about an hour and a half long. Mos Def was an amazing host, and the poets inspired Yahkira to even get closer to Marcus. After the show, they went to dinner at a famous steak house. Yahkira was fully enjoying herself when Marcus decided to take her home. She wasn't ready to end this perfect night. Marcus pulled into her driveway and parked. That's when Yahkira looked in Marcus's eyes and asked, "Would you like to come in?" Marcus had business to attend to; he had to go over Beth's house to check out how many clients had to be satisfied. He figured that those women couldn't give him want Yahkira could furnish him with: love. So he took her by her hand and said, "I would be delighted to see your home."

Yahkira lived with her mom, who was out for the entire night, so she was going to take full advantage of this perfect occasion. They went inside as Yahkira directed the way. She went into the kitchen and got some of her mom's Grey Goose vodka with two large wine glasses. Marcus got himself comfortable by sitting on the couch. Yahkira popped in a movie and sat very close to Marcus. They watched Friday, starring Ice Cube and Chris Tucker. She couldn't stop looking at Marcus's handsome features as she sipped on some more wine. He looked at her admiring him. Their eyes drew them closer, like a magnet, until they're lips were touching. Yahkira closed her eyes as Marcus's tongue went staggering in and out of her mouth.

She grabbed Marcus's hand and pulled him upstairs. They went inside her room, holding each other very firmly. Marcus simply asked her, "Are you sure that you want to do this?"

Yahkira looked him straight in his eyes while unbuckling his Steve Madden slacks and said, "More than anything in this world."

Yahkira took off her Gucci shirt and pulled down her skirt very slowly. She was standing there in a Victoria's Secret thong with the matching bra. Marcus watched her and got more excited as she directed him with her finger to get on the bed. He got on the bed and kissed her on her navel. He went down to her lower thigh and slowly pulled down her tiny underwear. He went even lower and went for her most precious part on her body. After the way his clients reacted to his tongue's stroke, he felt that he would get her wide open early.

Marcus put his tongue so deep inside her that she took her hands and started digging into the bed sheets.

"Oh shit, right there. Don't stop, oh my Goddd!" Yahkira howled out as Marcus did this circle rotation with his tongue that made her cum instantly. He sucked on her for nearly an hour. She came so many times she lost count.

Marcus just managed to put on a condom as Yahkira nearly jumped on his massive penis. She twirled in the bed, wanting to return the favor, but before doing so, he had already united his penis with her insides. He went very slowly as she started moaning upon entry, and it went from a moan to calling out his name at full volume. "Ohhh, Marcusss!"

He went gradually by lifting his ass up in the air, then making it go back down. His body was fully pressed against her soft, silky skin. He increased the pace, as he felt that he was about to detonate. Marcus looked her in her eyes and wanted to tell her he was falling in love with her already. That's when Yahkira yelled out, "Oh baby, I am about to cum again! Oh my god, Marcus! Baby, Marcusss!" They came at the same time, and they held each other until they fell to sleep.

Chapter Fifteen

King was putting in overtime with his clients. He was taking care of business, as he kept satisfying his ladies. King's clientele consisted to one of the top executives all way down to the secretaries. He was just thousands away from thirty grand to pay his lawyer.

Mary's sister, Marsha, went to Satisfier.com to set up a date with Marcus for next week. She just couldn't take her husband not being flattering in bed anymore, and she wanted what her sister had: multiple organisms. Marcus always liked to go on a date first before taking care of his ladies. He figured that was the best way to open them up and made them fill that they was in a safe environment when being around him.

Marsha was meeting Marcus for their date at Friday's restaurant. He waited for his client as he sipped on some peach Vodka. A young white woman walked in wearing dark shades and a scarf around her neck. She observed Marcus sitting at a table by himself and made her way over to him. She took a seat and introduced herself,

"Hi, my name is Marsha." She took her shades off, revealing her identity. Marcus couldn't believe his own eyes.

He blinked a couple of times to see if his eyes were working correctly.

"Was this the prosecutor that was handling King's case?" he asked himself. Marcus thought this was too good to be true. Marcus wanted to ask her, Aren't you that same bitch who's trying to send my friend to jail for the rest of his life? But he restrained himself from doing so. He also noted that she was wearing a big-ass rock on her finger. That's when he realized that this could work out to King's advantage. He did his normal routine by ordering their meal and some alcohol and telling her his price.

After they ate, just like her older sister, she was ready for satisfaction. Marsha was halfway drunk when they got to the hotel. She had no idea what she was getting herself involved in. Marcus tried to figure out how could he blackmail her to let King off in his murder case.

When Marsha went to the Web site, she didn't realize that King was actually Brian Jackson, who she was prosecuting. All the black criminals looked the same to her anyway, so she didn't care. She just wanted what her sister encountered: Marcus's tongue. So she paid no attention to King's half-naked picture that was posted throughout the Web page.

Marcus told Marsha that he was going to get some wine and would be right back. Marcus took out his cell phone and instantly dialed Beth's house, hoping that King was there. Beth answered the phone and told him that King was out pleasing one of his clients. Beth felt that Marcus had something really important to tell him, so she told him that she would have King call him as soon as he got in.

Marcus got back to the hotel room with some white wine and some flowers. Marsha was completely naked when he got back in the hotel's room. Marcus thought to himself,

"She is a sexy-ass white woman! Unlike Mary, her breast was small and perky. I might enjoy this after all."

Marcus bought a disposable camera that he kept in his coat pocket. He took another sip of wine and went right to work.

Marsha was so drunk as Marcus sucked on her neck. He put two fingers inside her ready-to-go vagina. She pulled down Marcus's pants and bent down to grab his huge dick and put all of him in her mouth. He thought to himself, "Damn, she is a freak!"

Marcus wanted to do something he had never done before. He thought this was a perfect opportunity, and it would definitely help out his plan. He had a few supplies that he carried with him on every trip: some motion lotion, some condoms, and KY Jelly. He turned her body around and put some of the jelly on the condom and inserted it in the vacancy of her ass. Marsha started screaming. After a few strokes, she started to relax and she took it like a professional. After a few hours of rough sex, Marsha was exhausted and fell asleep on the bed ass-naked.

Marcus took out his disposable camera and took quite a few pictures of her. He got dressed and went outside the room to try to get King on the phone again. King answered the phone and Marcus explained, "You will never guess who I just got finished satisfying."

Chapter Sixteen

Marcus sat in the dark as he waited patiently for Marsha to wake up from her deep sleep. An hour would go by before Marsha opened up her eyes. She glanced at Marcus sitting patiently in the dark. That's when she complemented him on his work.

"That was so wonderful! In all my wildest dreams I never experienced something that good before! How much do I owe you?"

"Since I gave you the full service, that will be twenty-five hundred dollars," Marcus responded.

Marsha got dressed and paid him the money he asked for. Marcus said to her right before she left, "See, I know that you are the district attorney for the superior court."

Marsha shut the door and said, "Excuse me?" Marcus explained.

"You is a smart lady and you also have a case sitting on your desk that you are handing: Brian Jackson. Well, the way I see it, and looking at the size of that ring on your finger, somebody out there loves you dearly."

"You son of a bitch. What makes you think anybody will believe your ass?" Marsha retorted.

"I got that covered, too. I have this camera and maybe I took some pictures of you being drunk and ass-naked."

"Are you trying to blackmail me, Mr. Slick?" Marcus explained to her the reason he took the pictures. "I need you to have Brian Jackson's case dismissed or these pictures will be floating everywhere imaginable."

Marsha had no choice but to listen to his proposal. She didn't know how she was going to do it, but what she did know was that her career and her marriage were in great jeopardy if she couldn't find a way to get that case dismissed. At that moment, Marcus felt as though he was the slickest man on this planet. He figured that he should be called Marcus no more, and be known as Slick since all his clients knew him as that anyway.

Marcus drove to Beth's house and couldn't wait to give King all the details. King came to the door, and Marcus told him the whole story. They jumped in Beth's Jeep and went to get the pictures developed. Marcus told King he gave her his cell number and expected to hear from her in the next twenty-four hours.

They went back to Beth's house and decided to chill out over there for the rest of the night. King looked over the pictures very closely. He couldn't believe that it was really the same prosecutor that was trying to lock him up. His prayers were answer. He thought to himself, "Who would of figure that the DA would pay for some dick?"

"Damn, I wish that I seen these pictures before I gave that hungry-ass lawyer the rest of the money," King said while observing the rest of the pictures.

"I tried to call you but you was tied up, but I didn't tell you the best part. Why did she take it in the ass like a pro," Marcus said while laughing at the job he done.

The next morning they waited apprehensively for Marsha's phone call. A private number appeared on Marcus's cell phone, and he answered it while putting it on loudspeaker. He wanted King to listen in on the conversation.

"Who is this?"

"It's Marsha. Listen because I can't speak long. Your friend is facing some serious charges, and the state has an eye witness who said he was the shooter. The best I could do is delay the trail's date and give you the information of the witness."

"That will be cool," Marcus responded.

She gave them the information that she had on file. Right before she got off the other end of the phone, Marcus asked her, "I hope this don't stop you from seeing me?" Marsha hung the phone up as the two of them busted out laughing.

Chapter Seventeen

Marsha was so embarrassed that she didn't tell her sister what happen. So Mary still required Marcus's services. Marcus was making anywhere from ten thousand to twenty thousand dollars a week by taking care of his ladies every day. Marcus and King started to establish a healthy bankroll.

King traded in his 2002 Cadillac for a pearl-colored 2003 CLK Mercedes Benz to match the year. He decked this car out with TVs in the headrests and twenty-two-inch custom rims. Even though he was being hunted by the Shottas and preparing to go to trail for murder, he felt that he was untouchable.

King felt that his case was already won after he made the witness an offer he couldn't refuse. As for the Jamaicans, they could run down on him if they wanted to. King told himself that they would end up just like their bubby, Devon. He bought a brand new handgun and a Tafton's bulletproof vest from Kenny's man. He made sure that he wore both everywhere he went.

King was making some serious money. He was charging his clients a range of five thousand to ten thousand dollars a night. King was making about fifty to a seventy-five grand a week. He was able to put Marie and her family in a house outside of Philly. Beth was the mastermind behind it all. She made a lot of money by getting a percentage off every woman that needed to be fulfilled.

Marcus still drove around in the '87 Caddy, wanting to keep his low profile. He gave Yahkira some jewelry and bought her some shoes. She was pretty much satisfied. She just figured he was still working at the warehouse and putting in a lot of overtime. Marcus left that job as soon as he took care of Mary.

Redd had no clue what his friends had been up to. They both kept him in the dark, thinking that he wouldn't approve of what they were doing. Redd was a hard-working man like his pops, and cheating on Layla was probably out of the question for him. Even though she cheated on him a few years back, Redd was a family man and you couldn't tell him otherwise, and besides, they didn't want to get him involved in that type of lifestyle.

Meanwhile Marcus sat at a restaurant in a black silk shirt waiting for a new client to meet him. A black elderly lady walked in and noticed Marcus sitting down at a table. She walked over to him and sat down at his table. Marcus thought she was just lost, because she was just to old to be trying to get her freak on.

"Hi, Slick, I'm hear for a date."

When she said that, Marcus simply got up and said, "You are old enough to be my grandma, lady," and started to walk away.

The old lady said, "At least hear me out. I'm willing to pay you twenty thousand dollars."

Marcus stopped in his tracks and turned around. "Twenty thousand dollars to do what?" Marcus said while sitting back down.

"What do you think about bringing my wildest fantasy alive?"

Marcus told the waiter to bring him a whole bottle of Hennessey.

When they got to the hotel, the old lady told Marcus she was going to the restroom to get prepared for him. Marcus thought to himself, "What people would do for money?"

She came out in nothing but a bathrobe and got on top of the bed. She opened up the robe and her breasts were huge with these enormous nipples. Marcus took another sip of Hennessey and slowly took off his silk shirt. And then he proceeded to take off his slacks in slow motion. He got on the bed and got right next to her; he spread her legs wide apart and took a deep breath. Before he knew it, he had his entire face between her floppy thighs.

Chapter Eighteen

King called the witness and told him who he was. The man was shocked that the man he was going to testify against was calling him on his cell phone. The man knew, if King had his cell phone number, then he probably had his address as well. So he agreed to meet him downtown in Chestnut. King told him that he would pay him fifty thousand dollars if he would disappear, and he gladly accepted the bait. King called up Redd and told him that he needed a favor from him. Redd was to be dressed in a half an hour to go with him downtown.

King needed somebody to go with him to pay his star witness a visit. He didn't know who this witness was and what he was capable of doing. Redd could be his muscle while he did the transaction and paid him off.

Redd hadn't seen King since the night he made bail, and he had a lot of questions to asked his friend. Redd been spending most of his time with Layla and his son. He got into King's CLK and wanted know how could he afford a car like this. The second question he had on his mind was, What was this favor he needed from him? Redd got in the Benz and got comfortable on the leather seat while King popped in a flick in his DVD player. It was starring himself and a client that he was satisfying. Redd sat there and wondered why was King wearing a bulletproof vest and who in the hell this white lady he was having sex with.

That's when Redd came to the conclusion that King was into something heavy, and having him go downtown made him even more suspicious. They got to the meeting spot and King told Redd, "You see that man standing over there? Well that's supposed to be the eye witness that claims I shot those two guys. This what I need from you. I need you to go over there and see if he is wearing a wire for the police."

Redd hesitated at first, but he did what King asked. He was really nervous when he first approached the man. He told him he had to pat him down in case he was wearing a wire. After checking him out, Redd gave King the word, letting him know that he was clean. King got out his car and walked toward them with a suitcase.

King told him that he was going to pay him twenty thousand now and that he would get the rest of the money when his case get dismissed. He also warned him that, if the police ever found out about this little meeting, he had his address as well as his parent's address. King ensured him that one of his goons would pay them a visit. The witness saw firsthand that he was capable of murder, and he didn't wanted his family to be harmed, so he took his word very seriously.

Six months went by until King's pretrial date. Marsha felt that she gave him enough time to delay his murder case. Now with no witnesses or evidence, she had no reason to go on with the trial. After the district's attorney made her closing statement, the jury was ready to deliberate their decision. One jury member passed the results to the sheriff, which he passed to the judge. He read the results out loud as the court remained silent.

"Without the state eye witness and no weapon found on the suspect, we had no choice but to find Brian Jackson not guilty of all charges."

King showed no emotion over the jury's decision. He sat there as if he didn't know what the verdict was going to be. King had Beth prepared the thirty grand for the witness like promised. He was going to meet him at same spot as before to give him the rest of the money.

Action News was there for the court's decision.

"The verdict is in and Brian Jackson is a free man, as the camera watches him giving his family a hug, a huge sign of relief."

King asked Marcus if he wanted to go with him to give this man the rest of the money, referring to the eye witness. Marcus told him that he had a client to take care of and that they would celebrate his victory later on tonight.

"Be careful and I see you really soon," Marcus told his friend while giving him another hug.

King got in the passenger side of Beth's Jeep and they got on Board Street and headed toward downtown. King noticed the same man waiting at the same spot as before. He got out and headed toward him. He gave him the suitcase with the rest of the money. King told him the next time he saw him again he wouldn't be too friendly. He got back in the Jeep, telling himself it was finally over.

A black van came out from nowhere and slammed its brakes by the side of the Jeep. The side door swung open with three guys jumping out wearing black ski masks, all loaded with machines guns. Before King or Beth knew what was going on, the men started firing. The sound of thunder ripped through the downtown area. The men jumped back in the van and peeled off.

King got shot so many times he didn't know if he was alive or dead. He turned to the driver's side and saw that Beth was crouched over with a fatal gunshot wound to her head. He managed to get his door open and made it to the ground, clasping for air to try to stay alive. King's bloody body could hardly move as an unidentified car pulled up. A man got out of the car with these long dreadlocks. He walked up to King and kicked him over so he could face him. King was hardly breathing when he noticed who it was: Floyd Lenox. He spoke with a deep Caribbean accent.

"So rube-boy, how long did you think you could run from me? Oh yeah, congratulation for beating your case boye."

He pulled out a .38 caliber Glock hand gun and put it up to King's forehead and squeezed the trigger.

Chapter Nineteen

Marcus was over Yahkira's house trying to relax from a long day at work. He felt that something was wrong because King hadn't called him the entire day. His cell phone rang and Redd's name appeared. He quickly answered the phone, and Redd was very quiet.

"Redd, what's wrong? Tell me what's going on?" Marcus sensed that Redd had some bad news to tell him, and he was right.

Redd told him that King and Beth were brutally murdered. Marcus dropped the phone and yelled out, "I knew it. I should have went with him. It was all my fault. I should have been there for him." He fell to the floor and started crying hysterically.

Yahkira grabbed him and tried to calm him down. She hugged him and was afraid to ask him what happened after seeing how upset he was. She already knew what it was without him saying a word. It was written all over his face. Marcus was hurt and had a good idea about his best friend's killer. He wanted revenge and he told himself that Denosh and her father were going to pay. Marcus realized that Redd was still on the phone.

He pick up the phone and told Redd that he should have been there. Redd explained that if he was there he wouldn't be alive right now. Marcus didn't look at it that way but knew that Redd was probably right.

Marcus knew that the satisfying business was over for sure. Without Beth setting up dates with the ladies from her job, there was no way that he could get in contact with his clients.

Marcus left Yahkira's house and drove to Turnersville and headed to Beth's house. When he got there, he was shocked that King's Benz was out front of her house. Marcus knew that the police would be there soon and tried to locate Beth's family. They would confiscate all her belongings, including anything that belonged to King. So he had to act fast. Marcus looked under a flowerpot where he knew that they kept a spare key to the house. He unlocked the door and went in the house. Marcus searched the entire house looking for one thing: King's money. He searched Beth's bedroom and noticed that there was a Nike box tucked away in the closet.

He open up the box and it was full of cash, a black book, a Mercedes title, and a Tec-Nine hand gun. He closed the box and went downstairs. He noticed that an extra set of Mercedes keys was sitting next to a laptop computer, and he grabbed them both. Marcus got in his car and drove about three blocks before he parked. He quickly walked back to Beth's house and got in the Benz. He opened up the laptop and saw all the information of the ladies he and King had satisfied in the past. He looked in the sky and said,

"King, I am going to do this for you." Marcus started up the Benz and drove off.

Chapter Twenty

Marcus looked through the black book and search for Marie's name. He found her name and slowly dialed her number. She answered the phone, and he told her the bad news about King. That's when Marcus found out that King had a son on the way. He immediately called Redd and told him he'd be over to his house in half an hour. Marcus figured that Redd was entitled to get some of the money, and hopefully he could get some of these clients. He was going to take a chance and see if he wanted to be involved with this type of business, which King had left behind.

Marcus went to his apartment and counted the money that was in the Nike box. He counted out three hundred thousand dollars in cash. He put a hundred thousand dollars to the side for Redd, so he could get himself straight. Marcus already had about two hundred thousand that he had accumulated over his period of time of satisfying his clients. With Beth's laptop, he was going to do his best to make a million dollars. He grabbed the car keys and headed to Redd's house.

He was shocked when Marcus pulled up in King's Benz. He got in and asked, "Marcus, Slick, tell me what's going on?"

"What I am about to tell you is going to blow your mind!" Marcus explained the entire story. He told him he had a lot of King's money, the title to his car, a gun, but most importantly Beth's computer.

"Beth's computer. What you going to do with a computer—go back to college?" Redd questioned him sternly.

"Well this car and all this money came from ladies that paid King to make their fantasies come true," Marcus said while headed back to Turnersville. He wanted to pick up the '87 Caddy that he parked a few blocks from Beth's house. He did that in case the police had already arrived at Beth's house. Redd quizzed Marcus on what he said.

"Bring out their fantasies. Do you mean have sex with them?"

"That's exactly what I mean, and this computer is what Beth was using to set up the whole thing. I even got me some ladies that were paying me to satisfy them. King called us, the satisfiers."

Redd was upset that he waited until King had died before telling him all this. It was a lot to take in, and now that King was dead he didn't know if he wanted to get involved, but he didn't tell Marcus how he felt. Marcus gave him the money and the '87 Caddy. He told him he would call him later in the evening.

After paying for King's funeral, Marcus knew that there was work to be done. By the way Redd reacted to what Marcus had told him about the satisfying business, he didn't know if he wanted to do it or not. So he planned to do it by himself and get paid. The first thing he did was redesign the Web page by putting up "Rest in Peace, King and Bethany." He figured the ladies all felt sorry for her, but life had to gone on. A few weeks went by and Marcus hasn't received one e-mail on the Web site.

Marcus and Yahkira got even closer since King's death. He had money and nothing but free time. He decided to take her to Atlantic City to the 2004 jazz festival that was taking place at The House of Blues. After that they went to Showboat casino to gamble for a bit and eat dinner in one of their most famous restaurants. Yahkira started falling in love with him. They went on the boardwalk for a nice evening walk. The sky was clear and the ocean was calm while they held hands and walked to the end of the boardwalk.

Yahkira noticed that Marcus was carrying more money on him than usual. Everywhere they went he left a huge tip. She didn't believe that the CLK was King's, and all the jewelry he bought her were some expensive pieces. She looked in Marcus eyes and asked, "Marcus what is it that you do?" Marcus was caught off guard. He couldn't tell her that he was still working in the warehouse, because the engagement ring in his pocket was worth at least five months of a warehouse's salary. He simply told her.

"Baby, after I left your house that night, I first found out about King and his girlfriend's murders. I drove over to Turnersville, where they were staying at, and got all their money they had stashed in a sneaker box. It was a lot of money, so I gave some to Redd."

Yahkira knew that King was in something illegal and had gotten Marcus involved. She told him that she didn't want him to end up the way King did.

They went back to the casino and got themselves a suite with a Jacuzzi in it. After taking a romantic bath, they gave each other a passionate massage with some baby oil. Yahkira grabbed Marcus's hand and said, "Tonight let's make love."

Marcus responded back to her by saying they could do that, but first he had something important to ask her. He went to his jacket and got out a small black box. Marcus went up to her and got on one knee and proposed.

"Yahkira, will you marry me?"

"Oh, my god! Yes, yes I will marry you!" They started kissing and all that night they made love.

Chapter Twenty-One

Marcus went home and figured that he couldn't satisfy these ladies forever. He wanted a regular life, and if Yahkira ever found out what he did for money, the marriage would be over before it even got started. That's when he decided to open up a night club.

Marcus was calling Redd up all day since he got back from Atlantic City. Redd's phone was disconnected, and his father hadn't heard from him in weeks. Marcus went to Layla's house and nobody answered the door. Redd was nowhere to be found.

It turned out that Redd couldn't live the life of having sex with different types of ladies to earn money. He took the hundred thousand that Marcus gave him, gathered his family, and left without a trace. Marcus was hurt once again because another one of his good friends left him hanging. Marcus wasn't upset with him though, because he understood that Redd had a family he had to look after.

Marcus looked at the Web page to see if any ladies needed taking care of, and their weren't any messages. Marcus finally realized that Beth's death played a major role in the Web page not getting recognition. All the women felt that Beth was dealing with killers and ended up getting herself killed.

Marcus felt that the night club would be a perfect move now. He only wished that there was some way to get in contact with Redd so he could tell him what his plans were. He had over four hundred grand in his possession, and planned to make a fortune.

Renee heard what kind of business King and Marcus were in. One of the girls that worked at the Comcast tower who knew this girl that sister knew Renee and she gave her the web page address. She typed in *www.satisfier.com* and there it was: Slick's half-naked picture. It read *"The man they call Slick can make you cum without his dick."* She printed out a copy and headed to Yahkira's house.

Renee wanted to personally deliver the bad news to Yahkira. Renee showed Yahkira the printed page and her heart just dropped. She was mostly upset that Marcus had lied to her. She didn't know how many women that he had had sex with, but she did know they had unprotected sex that night in Atlantic City. Yahkira sat on her bed and cried all night.

Marcus called Yahkira and noticed that she was crying her heart out. That's when he asked, "Baby what's wrong?"

"You bastard. You lied to me. I seen your Web page. You make bitches cum without using your dick? You can take this ring and go to hell!" She hung up the phone on him.

Marcus didn't know how she found out, but he wanted to tell her that part of his life was now over. Marcus felt miserable and went to his parents' house for comfort. He gave his mom and dad a hug and went down to the basement. He got on the couch where he and his two closest friends used to hang out. He thought to himself, "Damn, we had been through a whole lot together. We talked about all our girls and how one day we all was going be rich together." Even though Redd had left Marcus, he felt that he was happy somewhere with the hundred grand he gave him. Marcus had four hundred thousand dollars that he was going to use to open up a club. **TO BE CONTINUED!**

The Satisfaction Maintained

With both of Marcus's closest friends not around, Marcus kept the satisfying going by opening up the hottest club in South Philly. With Floyd Lenox still running the streets, Marcus still wanted revenge for King's death.

Chapter Twenty-Two

It was beginning of the year 2005 and Marcus's nightclub was one of the hottest clubs in South Philly. Everybody that was anybody filled up the club every Saturday night. Club King's was a place to be if you wanted to run across some celebrities. The security was tight and the VIP seats were incredible. Marcus was now mingling with the stars. When people weren't clubbing in there, it was an exotic strip club.

Every girl wanted to be around him, and every guy wanted to know him. Marcus was becoming a well-respected icon in Philadelphia. The opening night, Power 99 hosted rap star Eddie Morris's birthday blast at Club King's and all the stars were out. With other big stars wanting to celebrate their birthday parties at Marcus's club, he started to rake in plenty of doe.

Marcus was living in a million-dollar mansion in Chester. He was driving around in a 2005 Range Rover, and he still had the 2003 CLK. He had the interior customized with King's name written in gold in the seats. He had the Pennsylvania plates designed to also read *King.* Along with those, he had a black Yukon and a 2004 ES 330 Lexus that he hardly drove.

A year had gone by and Marcus still hadn't heard from Redd. Redd was now living in Newark, New Jersey, and he had taken the hundred thousand and bought a small home for his family. Redd felt dishonored the way he left Philly. He left his friend without telling him the real reason why. Redd's son, who was now eight, needed a good role model. Running around town with different type of women was no way to raise his son. Even though he didn't want to tell Layla what his friend did for a living, he ended up telling her anyway. She convinced him that leaving Philly was the best thing he could have done, because a city where at least three or more people got murdered every day was no place to raise a family.

Living in Newark, which had a high crime rate as well, would be best because nobody knew him or his family. After the ordeal with King's witness last year, he knew what Redd looked like and he strongly believed that the witness had something to do with King's death.

Layla's cousin, who lived in Philly, told her all about Club King's.

This famous person was there and that famous person was there. That's all her cousin could gossip about: all the celebrities that went in and out of Club King's.

Marcus knew quite a few big-time players, and it seen like everybody just wanted to be in his presence. Marcus wore a platinum Cartier frame with these huge-ass, princess-cut diamond earrings that blinged a mile away. His one-hundred-and-twenty-two karat diamond necklace gave off an amazing sparkle, and both his hands and wrists were covered in more ice than a freezer could carry. Marcus had a personal bodyguard that he kept around him at all times.

Chapter Twenty-Three

Marcus ran a gentlemen's club Monday through Thursday nights. He had some of the baddest girls that worked for him. Marcus's most attractive girl came from down South. She brought in a lot of guys. She was so sexy girls came out to see Carmen perform. When Marcus found her, he knew that he had struck gold. Carmen was thick-boned and had a golden complexion with these big-ass titties. They said down South chicks ate well, and she was living proof.

The gentlemen's club brought in a different type of crowd than the nightclub did on the weekends. It brought in some of the biggest drug dealers in Philly, New Jersey, even some out of New York. So those days Marcus tightened up the security with metal detectors at every entry. Even undercover cops would sneak in the club once in a while to see what drug dealer they could catch dirty.

The other problems that Marcus had to worry about were with the dancers having sex in the club. Any girl that got caught fucking in the club was fired on the spot. Marcus knew that having sex was the whole reason that he was a successful club owner in the first place. He also knew, if prostitution was caught in his club, he was going to lose everything he had worked so hard for. So he played it safe and paid his girls very well. He made them keep any tips that they received for striping. Since he opened the club a year ago, he had only had to fire two girls for having sex.

All the dancers tried to seduce Marcus, and watching tits and beautiful women wearing nothing but a thong all night was very temping. Marcus was caught off guard a few times and fell for them. He had sex with a couple of girls back in his office to relieve his stress. Marcus knew that he made the best investment a man could possibly make. He also knew that King was watching over him from above.

Marcus had money to throw around, so he wanted to do something special for King's aunt, who still resided a few blocks away from his parents' house. Her daughters left her alone in that big house, so she had nothing but free time on her hands. Samkia, her oldest daughter, was living in Camden with two kids. Her baby's father was in and out of jail, so she was basically on her own. Helen's second daughter, Carla, was living in Boston. She went on to college and got a degree in teaching and later became a teacher for young adults.

So after Marcus was finishing up his afternoon, he made his way over to Helen's house. She was so shocked to see Marcus she almost cried. She hasn't seen him since King's funeral, remembering the days that Marcus used to come over her house to pick up her nephew for school.

"So how you been, Marcus?"

"I am all right, Ms. Helen, and yourself?"

They spent the whole afternoon reminiscing about the good old days. Marcus gave her an envelope with a hundred thousand dollar check before leaving.

Chapter Twenty-Four

One Thursday night, the gentlemen's club was packed with wolves searching for young, beautiful dancers to feast on. The girls shook their asses around poles and on guys throughout the night. DJ Vas, who was one of the hottest DJs in Philly, put on Fifty Cent's "In the Club," and the dancers went crazy. Marcus watched the money flow in as he thought about the first time King popped in one of Fifty's mix tapes and told him that he was going to be huge one day.

Marcus walked around the club with Kare Davis, a.k.a. KD, at his side. KD been to prison for four years, and he was about five feet and nine inches tall. He weighted two hundred pounds and was all muscle. They made sure that the liquor kept pouring and the girls kept dancing. Marcus noticed a man yelling at his number one stripper from across the club.

"Fuck you, bitch. You ain't all that anyway!" the man screamed at Carmen. Marcus and security went over there to see why this man was harassing his employee. Marcus asked the guy, "What seems to be the problem?" The man snapped at Marcus. "This bitch took my money and only danced through half the song!" Marcus looked toward Carmen and asked if that was true.

"This prick is an asshole, and he tried to put his dirty-ass fingers in me, so I stopped dancing," Carmen responded.

Marcus told him that he had to leave his club and to never show his face in his club ever again. After Marcus said that, he got violent. He started cursing and yelling. Marcus noticed that everybody was watching him in action. So Marcus gave KD the word.

KD walked up to him and punched the man in the back of his head very hard. He knocked him out cold and the man collapsed to the floor. Security dragged him to the front entrance and threw him out on the sidewalk. They told the police that he was drunk and acting like a fool in the club. Marcus was sending a message to everybody in the club not to mess with his girls.

DJ Vas started up the music and the exotic dancers started shaking their asses. At about four in the morning, the club started to empty out. Marcus was sitting in his leather recliner counting money that the club made that night. Carmen was the last girl to leave and told Marcus she was about to leave for the night.

"I wanted to thank you for taking care of that asshole earlier," Carmen said with a voice that could seduce the President.

"That was nothing. If you fuck with one of my girls, that's what going to happen every time," Marcus responded.

Carmen walked in the door and locked it behind her. She went up to him and said, "Is their anything I can do for you before I leave?"

Marcus was sipping on some Moet and put his hand on his chin. He went over to his personal bar and got a wine glass for her. He poured some Moet in the glass and asked her, “What made you get into this type of business? I am going to tell you the truth. You’re too pretty to be doing this line of work.” Marcus was now worth millions and telling her the truth wasn’t too hard. At first Carmen thought Marcus was just in it for the money and didn’t give two shits about anything else. After talking to him for a while, she wanted him more than ever.

Carmen stood up and took off her leather jacket. She unbuttoned her blouse, revealing her huge breasts. She proceeded to take off her leather skirt and stood in front of him in just a thong. She went up to Marcus and sat on his lap. She started kissing him on his neck while putting her hand inside his pants. Carmen caressed him very tenderly, making Marcus quickly get stimulated, and that’s when she said, “Damn, with a dick this big, I should be paying you.” Marcus grinned and thought, “If only she knew the half of it.” She looked at him as he laid back in his recliner and went to work on his large masculinity, which she was so affectionate toward. She massaged him very tenderly, making him jerk just a little, loving it at the same time. She dug in her purse, putting her hand on a shiny wrapper, and pulled out a Ruff’s Rider condom. She ripped it open with her teeth and smoothly placed the condom on her tongue. She efficiently placed the condom on Marcus’s penis with her warm mouth. She moved her thong to the side and sat on Marcus from the behind, making his cock easily slide inside her. She went all the way down and slowly lifted her voluptuous ass back up; she did this gyrating rotation that made her ass bounce against his hairy sacks. Marcus sat there and enjoyed every moment of it.

After a few hours went by doing every position possible, Marcus was ready to climax. She felt that his legs were getting really stiff; she jumped off him and quickly took the condom off. She put the head of his manly hood inside her mouth and jerked the rest of his dick with her hands. Marcus came very hard inside her mouth, making him completely satisfied.

Chapter Twenty-Five

Marcus had Carmen stop dancing and put her in charge of the other dancers. The girls envied her because she accomplished what they had been trying to do for a whole year. Marcus also had Carmen help him run the nightclub on the weekends. Marcus felt like a real king that was sitting on top of the world.

When Yahkira found out that Marcus owned Club King's, she was stunned. The only man that she had truly loved was a successful club owner. She knew that Marcus probably got that club from having sex with all types of different girls. She hated the fact that he had lied to her, but she felt that he deserved another chance. Besides, she couldn't stand around doing nothing while Marcus was making all this money and she couldn't get any. So she decided to go to the club with her girls the following Saturday night.

It was Saturday night and the streets were filled with luxury cars and young people all trying to get into Club King's. The ladies hardly wore anything, while the guys wore all types of throwback jerseys with the matching fitted cap. The police patrolled the area searching for anything they could find. Yahkira, Renee, and two other girls searched for a parking spot.

One of the girls with Yahkira spotted a parking space and told Renee to park there. Yahkira had this glamorous Baby's Phat outfit that made every guy that went by her try to holla. She had one thing on her mind and that was finding Marcus.

The ladies got in the club for free so they had their own line. Yahkira and the rest of the girls were in Club King's in no time. The club was packed as usual, and both dance floors was pumping. Yahkira looked around to see if Marcus was anywhere in sight. Marcus was in the back counting money as KD stood by the door.

Carmen hosted the party and made sure everything ran smoothly. Yahkira and Renee went up to the dance floor while the other girls stayed at the bar. Some dude asked Renee if she wanted to dance and she gladly accepted, leaving Yahkira to dance by herself. Some light-skinned kid went up to Yahkira and said, "Damn, girl, you're fine as hell! May I get this dance?" She didn't want to miss Marcus, so she told him not right now. She knew that there were a lot of ballers in the club, but you weren't really balling until you owned your own club.

It had two floors with DJ's on both floors playing two different types of music. The VIP section was miraculous with comfortable seats. It had a marble floor that probably cost a fortune. Yahkira admired how electrifying this club actually was. She thought to herself that Marcus had really come up.

That's when Marcus walked out with KD at his side. Yahkira noticed him across the room and tried to make her way over to him. Everybody shaking his hands and speaking to him made Yahkira even more coveted. By the time she made her way through the mob of people, Carmen was already wrapped around his arm.

Yahkira knew that some lucky girl was going to snatch him up. He was flossing with so many diamonds it made it really hard not to recognize him. He had KD at his side making sure nobody got to close to him. She didn't want to seem like a groupie, so she decided not to approach him right off bat. Yahkira went to the bar where her other two friends were sitting and watched Marcus from a distance. One of the girls said, "Go and get him if it's like that," not knowing that was the man she was so close to marrying. It was about two thirty in the morning and the club started to empty out. Renee and the other girls were ready to leave, and Yahkira still hadn't had a chance to speak to Marcus. Yahkira figured it just wasn't her time, so she also decided to call it a night. That's when Marcus realized that he knew that face from anywhere.

Chapter Twenty-Six

Marcus told Carmen he would be right back. He went over to Yahkira with KD right behind him, and her face lit up when she saw Marcus headed her way.

"Yahkira, how are you?" Marcus asked while giving her a hug.

"I am fine and I can see that you are doing really well for yourself," Yahkira responded while not trying to admire his jewelry. Renee sucked her teeth at Marcus as she waited patiently for her friend. The other two girls just wanted to know why in the hell he was talking to her. Yahkira was so caught up in the moment she didn't realize that her friends started hating on her. Marcus wanted to tell her how much he missed her and also tell her that he didn't mean to lie to her about how he made his income. Right before doing so, he was rudely interrupted by Renee.

"Come on girl, so we can go get something to eat."

"I see that your friends are in a rush, but take my card and call me someday," Marcus said while handing her his business card.

Yahkira took the card and told him right before leaving, "I really did miss you." She and the rest of her entourage left the club, and she was delighted that he spoke to her. Renee was upset at her for talking to him, still thinking that he was a dog.

"Why did you take that man card after what he did to you? He's nothing but a whore and he broke your heart in the past. What make you think he not going to break your heart in the future?" Renee commented, Yahkira didn't want to hear what she had to say, because she was going to have Marcus one way or another, whether Reene liked it or not. He was going to be her meal ticket out of the hood. The way Marcus treated her in the past made her feel like a real star. Even though Marcus sold himself on the Internet in the past, he was a successful club owner now, and he had plenty of money to prove it. So Yahkira didn't care what Renee thought about him.

Marcus invested his money all throughout Philly. He had about six houses that he rented out to people who were on section eight. That made him get his money on time with no problems. Marcus put the club and all his homes in his father's name and had his cars in his mother's name. He did this in case there was any reason he couldn't get to his assets; he would always have that to fall back on.

When the last person left the club that night, they were ready to put the locks on the doors. That's when four Jamaicans walked in wearing black suits. Marcus immediately noticed them and walked toward them with KD backing him up. One of them had these long dreads that were touching his back, and they all wore colorful bandanas. That's moment Marcus knew that they were with the Shottas Gang. The one with the longest dreads asked, "Who own this bloody club, mon?"

Marcus said, "That would be me. Who asking?"

"Is that right rube boy. Well my name is Floyd Lenox and I just wanted to congratulate you on your success."

The Rasta mon responded. By this time the rest of security arrived and the police were just outside.

They exited the club with no incidents. Floyd just wanted to know who would name his club after a person he murdered a year ago. He wanted to see who was in charge and would be so disrespectful toward the Shottas. That's when he decided whoever that man was just inherited King's beef.

Chapter Twenty-Seven

Marcus knew that this was going to happen sooner or later. Marcus was a rich man and he wasn't going to let this old-ass Jamaican run him from his little empire. Marcus had KD go around Philly to find the most ruthless and toughest guys that wanted to make some extra cash. KD got his cousin, who was a former gang member. Duke was from Southwest and was known for knocking niggas out. He recruited this other guy who was six foot nine and was a born killer. He went by the name of Mick. When he was twelve, he did time in the juvenile detention center for killing his father for allegedly beating on him and his mom. He was twenty-two now and he had just gotten out a month ago. So KD knew that Mick needed a job.

Marcus's cell phone rang and a 973 area code appeared. Marcus didn't recognize the number, but he answered it anyway.

"Who is this?' Marcus asked vividly.

"Marcus it's Redd." Redd was dead broke and Layla had left him with his son and went back to Philly a while ago. Redd wasn't working and the bank had just put his house up for sale. All Redd had to his name was the '87 Caddy that Marcus had given him a year ago.

"So what's up, Redd?"

"Nothing much, man. I am sorry the way I left Philly. My back was against the wall. I been staying in Newark, and that bitch took my son and went back to Philly," Redd explained, hoping that Marcus would have some type of sympathy for him.

That's when Marcus responded, "Man, forget about the past and let us focus on the future."

Redd felt relieved that Marcus didn't have hard feelings for his leaving him the way he did. Marcus told him to come back to Philly; he would have a job waiting for him.

Marcus needed a man that he could trust. He knew that Floyd was plotting something against him and his club. He had just hired four more guys to work for him that KD drafted. He held a meeting to see if these guys would be loyal and not afraid to bust a gun when the time came. Marcus told them that he was calling them the King's Squad. One of the dudes jumped up and simply asked, "Yo, how much are we're getting paid?" Marcus was an intelligent man and his nickname was Slick. He knew that the first man who asked about how much they were going to make was only in it for the money.

"What's your name, man?" Marcus quizzed him.

"Al Smooth," The kid responded.

Al Smooth was handpicked by Duke. Duke told KD that he was young but handled his business like a real soldier. They both ran with the same gang out of Southwest. When everybody in the gang ended up getting killed or locked up, they stuck together and ran the streets themselves. "Well, Al Smooth, is it? Since you going to be at the front door at all times, you're going to make five hundred a week," Marcus responded boldly to his question.

"Shit, that's all right with me!" Al Smooth said quickly. Marcus gave him a slight grin when he saw how excited Al was when he told him that. Marcus was ready to pay him two grand a week for just being a member of the King's Squad.

Redd finally arrived in Philly and was trying to find where Club King's was located. He pulled over and asked a group of girls that were walking by.

"How are y'all ladies doing? Do y'all know where Club King's is at?"

"You are talking about that club in South Philly," one of the girls answered him. Redd thanked her and headed to South Philly. He drove down South Street hoping that the club would just pop out at him. That's when he saw a building with a huge crown on it that read *Club King's*. Redd thought to himself, "This must be it! Damn, Marcus a club owner!" He parked and went up to the front entrance, only to be stopped by Al Smooth.

"The club doesn't open until ten, my man."

Redd explained that he was looking for his friend Slick. AL Smooth told him that he didn't know a Slick.

"Marcus. He the owner of the this club," Redd said while Al Smooth got on his Nextel and chirped Marcus.

"Yo, Marcus, I got some dude that says he knows you."

Marcus and KD came to the door to see who was looking for him.

Chapter Twenty-Eight

Weeks went by and there was still no word from the Shottas Gang. Marcus made Redd in charge of the security. KD was in charge of King's Squad, and Carmen was in charge of the strippers. Marcus was bringing in a hundred thousand a week. The other club owners started to see a decrease in their profits. Marcus knew that he didn't only have to worry about the Jamaicans. He also had other club owners trying to hurt his business. With his main man back in town, he was ready to take over the whole city.

Yahkira called up Marcus to tell him that people were going around saying that the Shottas were out to get him. She told him that one of her girl's cousins went out with one of the Shottas and he told her that Marcus was going to get what he deserved. He told her not to worry about that little-ass rumor. Marcus thanked her for her concern, and that's when he realized that she still had deep feelings for him. He told her that he was about to make a run to the bank and he would call her later.

Marcus jumped in the back of his Range Rover with King's Squad and headed to the bank. Marcus told Redd to keep security on high alert because Floyd Lenox was going to make his move soon. KD parked the Range Rover, and

Marcus went inside the bank to make a deposit. He got in line and seconds later all he heard was loud gunshots. Everybody in the bank fell to the ground, all thinking that the gunshots were in the bank. He immediately got up and ran to the Range Rover. He had seen that his SUV had about six bullet holes in it. Duke was leaking blood since he had caught a bullet in the left shoulder.

KD said to Marcus, "It was those fucking Jamaicans. I am telling you, we need to get ourselves some fucking guns!"

Police arrived minutes later to try to figure out what just happened. KD told the cops that he didn't knew who the hell was shooting at them. The ambulance arrived and assisted Duke with his shoulder.

Marcus was ready to take Floyd and his Shottas to war. They killed his best friend, and now they had shot up his new Range Rover. Marcus chirped Redd on his Boost Mobile phone and told him what happened and that he was taking the Shottas gang to war. Redd knew that this was going to happen. He thought to himself, "Well why not. I got nothing to lose. Layla took my son away from me, and I got to show Marcus that I'm still a loyal friend."

Marcus pulled up to the club and noticed that an unidentified black van parlaying in the cut (It was park just a few blocks away from his club.). Marcus walked by Redd and went right to his office. With the squad watching him, all waiting anxiously to see what his next move would be. Marcus went into his safe and pulled out a Tec-Nine that King had left behind. KD went in the office to see what Marcus wanted him to do.

Marcus handed him the gun and said, "Get one of those so-called soldiers of yours to see who's in that fucking van!"

KD went out and handed the gun to Mick and told him, "This is your chance to prove yourself to Marcus. Go and see who's in that black van."

Mick put on his black hoodie and went out the back door. He went up the block, then walked by the black van to observe who was in it. Just as Marcus had expected, it was two brethrens watching and plotting on the club, waiting patiently for their opportunity. They didn't notice the man who was wearing the black hoodie when he walked by the van. The Shottas were smoking on some of Floyd Lenox's gongja and couldn't see due to the thick smoke that was inside the van. Mick snuck up on the van and pulled out the Tec-Nine. He tapped on the passenger side window, and before he knew that he was doing so, he was squeezing the trigger.

Chapter Twenty-Nine

There was police investigating the crime scene that took place on South Street. Yahkira turned on her TV as Eye Witness News had a special report. The reporter stated all information the police had.

"Two men were violently murdered just a few blocks away from Club King's. The men were believed to be members of a ruthless gang. They were gunned down earlier this afternoon. There are no witnesses or evidence of the executioners. The police ask that anyone with information call Crime Stoppers."

Yahkira felt in her heart that Marcus had something do with all this. She didn't know if he had become a gangster or if these men just happened to get murdered a few blocks away from his club. She restrained herself from calling him that evening.

Floyd Lenox was furious when he found out about two more of his men getting killed. He held a meeting at his West Philly home and told all his soldiers to strap up (to carry guns). They were going to burn Club King's down.

Marcus, on the other hand, gave Mick twenty thousand for handling that for him. He was letting his other men know that they would be rewarded when they did something like Mick done. He made Mick lay low for a while in one of his six homes. Marcus wanted revenge, and killing two of Floyd men was only the beginning. Marcus had KD bring automatic weapons and made all his men carry one on them at all times. KD recruited more soldiers and had two of them armed with shotguns at the door. Marcus was taking no more chances with the Shottas.

The word on the streets was that Marcus was at war with Floyd Lenox. It started hurting Marcus's business but he could care less. All he wanted was Floyd Lenox's head on a platter. Marcus eventually closed down the club after it started costing more to run it than he was bringing in. He also figured that it made it easy for the Shottas to get at him. Marcus told his men whoever killed Floyd Lenox would be rewarded one hundred thousand dollars. That's all they needed to hear and they were ready to go to war with him.

Marcus and Redd laid low at his mansion in Chester while KD and rest of King's Squad went around the streets looking for any Shottas. Marcus went from a successful club owner to a ruthless mob boss, and Redd was his under boss. KD was the general of King's Squad, as he kept recruiting more and more soldiers. They were expanding across the city of Philadelphia. Marcus was becoming Mr. Untouchable.

Floyd had safe houses throughout the entire city, so it made nearly impossible to find him. He still brought in a lot of cash in from the streets and had over two hundred men that were part of his Shottas gang. Marcus didn't have the manpower or enough guns to take Floyd on. He just figured, if he couldn't get to him, then he would get to his people.

Months went by and the war got worst. Yahkira open up the newspaper and read, *"The streets are becoming more and more dangerous with two local gangs that are currently at war. Guys are popping up dead every day, and the two men that are believed to be responsible are nowhere to be found. Crime bosses Floyd Lenox and former club owner Marcus Smith. People believe that the war was started over Marcus's best friend, Brian Jackson, who was viciously murder nearly two years ago."*

Chapter Thirty

The FBI was trying to put a stop to this war that had left at least twenty men dead. Agent Carl Wilson and Agent Sam Nelson were assigned to this particular case. The mayor needed to put an end to this war because the election was coming up. The war was broadcasted on the news and every day the local newspaper wrote about it. People were afraid to leave their homes and didn't want to send their children to school.

They were arresting members from both gangs, trying to find the location of their bosses. With no success, they continued to patrol the streets. Marcus had properties all over Philly, and even though the feds wanted to talk to him, they couldn't pin anything on him. With plenty of cars and an endless amount of cash, Marcus could have left Philly a while ago. He had too much pride and always told himself that Floyd would one day pay for murdering King.

Floyd was a gangster, and going to war was what he knew. Everybody knew about the Shottas and knew that Floyd was the headman calling the shots. The police didn't know what he looked like, and he had never been arrested before. They tried to get some undercover cops in his organization, but they all were unsuccessful. Denosh went back to Jamaica last month. Right before she left, she had tried to convince her dad that it been enough bloodshed. She knew that this war was originally started because of her and couldn't stand the fact that all these men were losing their lives every day. Floyd wasn't going to back down from anybody, and he sure wasn't going to back down from some punk club owner.

Marcus gave KD the Range Rover for being his top-ranked solider and keeping all his men on point. Marcus kept all the soldiers on salary so they could feel satisfied. He sold the club for nearly a million dollars and the feds couldn't do shit about it. The club was under his dad's name anyway, as were the rest of his properties. They knew that he was the boss of King's Squad, but they couldn't prove it. Marcus wasn't involved in any drug activities, and he never did anything to get his hands dirty.

KD, Duke, and AL Smooth drove around all night in the Range Rover looking for some Shottas. After a few hours went by, they turned their search into trying to find some girls to holla at. They went to the West side, where they knew a spot that these girls hung out at. They were carrying loaded guns in case they had to approach some Jamaicans. Duke was recovering from his bullet wound in the shoulder, which occurred when the Shottas did the drive-by at the bank. They noticed two Jamaicans wearing suits, standing outside a vacated building. KD recognized one of them that were at the club that night. An older Rasta came out the building with really long dreads. KD circled around the block and thinking that the older Rasta looked really familiar. It came to him. He was Floyd Lenox. He told Duke that was definitely Floyd with the long dreads for sure. Floyd got in a black 500 Benz with a young female at the wheel.

They followed the Benz, waiting anxiously for the right moment. They were about three cars from the Benz when it came to a stop at a red light. Duke and Al Smooth jumped out, with Duke wearing an ace bandage on his left arm. Al Smooth pulled out his Glock while Duke released the safety off his AK-47. KD remained in the car while the two of them sneaked behind the Benz. The three cars that were in front of them all had passengers in them. They got up on the Benz and that when Floyd seen them and said, "You pussy-cock boyes want to rump with me!" He tried to reach for his gun, but it was to late. They emptied their clips on him and the young female. Floyd never had a chance; the girl died instantly. Floyd got shot about twenty times and the great Shottas' body was bleeding copiously as they tried to run back to the Range Rover.

The car behind the Benz had two Jamaicans in it that were supposed to be Floyd's bodyguards. Jumping out of the car, being to late to help their boss, both had loaded guns and started firing at Duke and Al Smooth. One of the Rastas caught Al right in the chest. He dropped to the ground holding his chest as Duke fired back. KD jumped out the Range with a sawed-off shot gun and crept behind one of the Jamaicans. Before he could turn around, KD pumped the gun twice and let off two shots in one of the Jamaican's backs. The other Jamaican seen that KD killed the other Shotta and started firing at him. He ducked behind a car while Duke inserted another clip in his gun. He stood up and unleashed his gun on the other Shotta, killing him with multiple gunshots.

KD and Duke got back in the SUV, leaving AL Smooth dead in the street. They drove off while leaving witnesses behind watching their every move. They didn't even get past a block and a squad car was behind them. KD put his foot to the medal, blowing past a few red lights and dodging cars through traffic. The cops were able to block them in. They were surrounded by cop cars with guns draw at them. They jump out and made a run for it. Duke pulled out his AK-47 and took the cops on. KD was boxed in and took cover behind a parked car. Duke started firing at the police, hitting two of them. He aimed at another officer, and before he could pull the trigger, a sharp shooter took him out. KD watched his cousin's life end and threw his gun toward the officers. He got down on his hands and knees saying, "Don't shoot! Don't shoot! I give up!"

Agent Carl Wilson and his partner Sam Nelson arrived on the scene and took Kare Davis into custody.

Chapter Thirty-One

Marcus and Redd watched Eye Witness News as the reporter stated, "Today crime boss Floyd Lenox was assassinated. Six are dead, including a police officer. As multiple gunshots spread through the streets of Philadelphia, the suspects fled the scene in a white sport utility vehicle while police tracked them down, killing one of the suspects before doing so. Later finding out that the suspect who was a minor, name is being withheld due to his age. The suspect shot and killed an officer and wounded another. The second suspect, identified as Kare Davis, was captured and charged with multiple murders, several weapons offenses, eluding the police, and several other charges. He is being held with no bail. He's believed to be a member of King's Squad and took order from this man." The news broadcasted Marcus's picture.

This was the first time that Marcus's picture was posted on the news. He knew that every police officer would be tracking him down.

Carl and his partner started to piece the clues together. Brian Jackson killed Floyd Lenox's nephew. Brian was believed to have been murdered downtown just after he was acquitted at his murder trail. Two of Floyd's men were murdered in a black van just a few blocks away from Club King's. A drive-by went down at Wachovia's Bank that placed Kare Davis, Duke, AL Smooth, and crime boss Marcus Smith. All these crime scenes were all connected. Marcus was connected to Brian, a.k.a. King, when he cosigned for him to make bail. That's why his club was named after him when he died. They had enough evidence to bring Marcus into custody. They just needed KD to say that he initiated the hit on Floyd Lenox.

"Mr. Davis, I got enough information to fry your ass, but I'm going to cut you a break. I am going to make you a deal that you can't refuse. You can walk away from all this doing ten or fifteen years in prison. All you got to do is tell me that Marcus was the man calling the shots. Marcus was the one who gave the hit for Floyd Lenox; am I right?" Agent Carl said while lighting him a cigarette.

KD was very loyal, but when they had him in that small room and were giving him a choice of life or death, it would make the toughest man fold under pressure. After thinking about his cousin being shot to death, he ended up giving them the information they needed. He told them that Marcus was the one calling the shots and had told him whoever murder Floyd Lenox would get paid a hundred thousand dollars.

The FBI issued a warrant for Marcus's arrest and searched for him at all his properties. He was now laying low at Carmen's house. He had heard about KD dropping the dime on him and knew that the cops would search his mansion in Chester.

Redd drove around in his new 2005 Bentley continental GT with Saffron interior that he just bought a month ago. He wore a platinum chain and had a pocket full of cash. Marcus was paying him rather well for being his right-hand man. He drove around to all six of Marcus's homes to collect the rent from all his tenants.

Marcus was on the run and was still making money. He had at least a million dollars in cash that was in a safe at his parents' house, and his mansion was worth a million dollars. He had two luxury cars and a fully-loaded Yukon that was all paid for. He could sell them if he needed some extra money.

Redd drove to German Town to collect the rent from the last house. Marcus was waiting to sell all his properties before he left Philly. Carmen stayed in Center City and Marcus made Redd drop off all the money over there. Redd figured, since Marcus was on the run, he had to step up and become the man. He turned on 22nd Street, and that's when he seen her. Layla was getting into a blue Honda Accord with T-Bone in the driver seat. T-Bone had the radio blasting and all his windows down, just knowing he was the shit. He was dark-skinned and his mouth was full of diamonds.

Redd pulled over to side of the blue sedan and stared right at her. Layla's mouth nearly dropped, and that moment she realized that she had made the worst mistake in her life. T-Bone noticed that Layla was all into Redd's new appearance. He took the backside of his hand and smacked the shit out of her.

"You what that nigga? Then get the fuck out of my car, bitch," T-Bone said while he grinned at Redd.

Redd reached underneath his seat and pulled out a 9mm handgun and cocked it back. He got out of his car and walked over to T-Bone. He put the gun right to his head and said to Layla, "Get in the car. You coming with me!"

T-Bone was furious, and he wasn't going out like any punk. He was mad as hell. The one day he leaves his gun in the house, some shit like this goes down. T-Bone said to him, "The next time I see you, it's on, so you better kill me now!" Redd laughed at him, while walking backward, still aiming the gun at him. He got back in his car and drove off.

Layla was completely shocked to see him in action and said to him, "Redd, I am so sorry how I left you in Jersey. We didn't have no money and—"

Redd cut her off by saying, "And that going to be enough. I'm taking you to your mom's house and that's it. I just couldn't have that nigga smacking on my babyma."

She knew that Redd was back in town and working for Marcus. She also knew that they were at war. It had been all over the news, and everybody talked about it.

"Well I heard what happen. The police are looking for Marcus for those shooting that happen on the West Side. I just want you to be careful out in these streets," Layla warned him. He looked at her and didn't stay another word.

Redd ended up dropping Layla off at her mom's house and headed to Center City. Agent Sam Nelson noticed Redd's Bentley driving by. Redd got to Carmen's house and tried to explain to Marcus what just happened. He quickly questioned Redd, "Did you get everybody rent?"

"I got mostly everybody, except the people in German Town. I ran into some problems with that cat T-Bone. He hated on me so I had to pull out my nine on his ass," Redd responded.

"Redd, listen very closely to me because you already know that I'm on the run and if you do something stupid then I got to be worried about your ass, too," Marcus said while looking out the window.

That's when he saw that the police had Carmen's house surrounded. They kicked in her door and said, "It's the FBI. We've got a search warrant for Marcus Smith."

Chapter Thirty-Two

Agent Carl and his partner Agent Sam arrested Marcus and took him downtown. Sam was relieved that his intuition about this Bentley had brought them to Marcus. They knew that, if a person in Philly was driving a new Bentley and they weren't Allen Iverson or Donna McNabb, then they were probably into something illegal. They had an unmarked cop car follow Redd, and just like Sam expected, it led them to their target. They didn't arrest Redd because they didn't have anything on him, and they didn't even know who he was. They got who they were looking for.

Yahkira hadn't heard from Marcus in months, and she almost fainted when she saw him on the front page of the newspaper. It read, *"Crime boss and organizer of the blood bath between two rival gangs, and the person that is believed to gave the word for the execution of Floyd Lenox are behind bars. They are holding him on a million- dollar bail."*

With Marcus in police custody, Redd was going to do whatever he had to do to get him out. He had Mick still laying low in one of Marcus's homes, and he had about four men left that still considered themselves King's Squad members. Carmen had two hundred thousands dollars of Marcus's money stashed away for him. Redd sold the

Bentley, the CLK, and Marcus's Lexus. He got the money that Carmen had stashed away for Marcus. Redd quickly got about five hundred thousands dollars. He drove Marcus's Yukon to Marcus's parents' house to see if they sold any of the houses. Marcus's dad foreclosed two of the homes and gave Redd four hundred and fifty thousand dollars in a certified check. Redd went to the jewelry store on Market Street and pawned his platinum chain. They gave him fifty thousand for it and Redd was heated.

"Damn, I nearly paid a hundred grand for that shit!" Redd said to the jeweler. He said "fuck it" because he had a million dollars in his possession and went to go bail his friend out of jail.

Marcus was starting to think that Redd had something to do with him being arrested, but after he was released and seen Redd in the lobby, that's when he knew he had a loyal friend.

He told him he had a million dollars in cash in a safe at his parents' house. He would hire Jerry McGinnis, the same Jewish lawyer that King had. Marcus felt betrayed because of what KD did to him. They got KD in that small room and he broke down. He called up Mick, who was still laying low, to inform him that he was the new leader of King's Squad. Even though they only had about four guys left in the squad, Marcus wanted everybody in Philly to know that King's name lived on. He insisted that Redd be the top man in charge until his legal problems were all over.

Marcus gave Redd a half of the million dollar that he had in his parents' basement. He told him to go to New Jersey and open up a Club King's. He said to take Mick and the rest of King's Squad with him in case of any problems. Redd and the rest of the King's Squad left that night in the '87 Cadillac.

Marcus took two hundred and fifty thousand and gave it to Jerry McGinnis. Since this was a high-profile case, he charged him a quarter of a million dollars to represent him. Marcus went to his parents' house to thank them for everything they did for him. Marcus gave them the four houses that were still in their names. He hugged them and told them not to worried about this bullshit case, to excuse his French. He left and headed to Center City. He noticed that Carmen got the door repaired, after the feds had left it off the hinges.

He knocked on the door and Carmen came to the door in her nightgown. She wasn't that shocked when she saw him. She knew it was just a matter of time until the police released him. She gave him a hug and a passionate kiss. They caressed each other and ended up having sex with neither one of them saying a word. Marcus told her right before leaving, "I am going to give you a hundred thousand dollars to hold for me. When this is all over, I'm going to take you to New Jersey with me." He gave her a kiss and headed to his Chester home. He hadn't been there for a while and he wanted to check to see if his million-dollar investment was all right. All he had in his name was his mansion, one hundred and fifty thousand in cash, and a black Yukon. He couldn't stop thinking that he was worth 3.7 million dollars before KD ratted him out. Marcus started his fortune from four hundred grand and he was determined to get it all back.

Chapter Thirty-Three

Six months later

Marcus got in his black Yukon and headed downtown for his first appearance in court. His two lawyers drove in front of him to answer all the press's questions. Marcus wore a tailored black business suit, a silk tie, and his hair was neatly done. When he arrived, he could see all the news vans that were lined up around the block. News reporters were out there with their cameramen. Microphones were set up, all waiting for a statement from Marcus Smith.

One reported noticed a BMW and a black SUV pulling up. She saw two men getting out with their briefcases and another man getting out of the black truck. That's when she told her cameraman to get ready because she just knew that was Marcus Smith. They approached the front doors of the court house and the news reporter asked, "So, Mr. Smith, how does it feel that one of your own is testifying against you?"

Marcus remained silent while his lawyer answered her question.

"Well I am sure that my client is innocent of all charges. The state witness was a former employee at my client's nightclub, but after being involved with a police officer death, he is trying to get out of a life sentence they presented him with. That will be all for the moment and once again my client is innocent."

They avoided any more questions and went inside the Supreme Court Building. Since Marcus had federal charges, he had to go before a supreme court judge.

Marcus's lawyers prepared theirs cases as the state got KD prepared to testify against his formal boss. The jury that was handpicked by Marcus's lawyer a week ago all waited patiently for the supreme court judge to come out.

That's when the sheriff asked everybody to please rise as the judge came out. She told everybody to have a seat. The judge was this old lady and had on a face that she had sent a lot of people away forever. She took her seat and told the district attorney to present the case. That's when Marcus looked at her very closely and noticed that this judge looked really familiar. He couldn't fucking believe it! He thought to himself that this was to good to be true. Was this the old lady that paid him twenty thousand dollars to get satisfied?!

Special Preview

The hand that I was dealt.

This book was written for gamblers, casinos employees, tourists, and anybody who wants to know how gambling can change your life forever!

Chapter One

My name is Bill Hamilton Junior, and I am twenty-two years old. The year was 2003 and I was finishing up my last year at Boston University. My major was Business Administration and I learned all I could about marketing and promotion. I'm from Egg Harbor City, a small town out of New Jersey. My father built a huge house and started a family there back in the eighties. The city had a population of about thirty thousand people, and it was just thirty minutes away from America's favorite playground. Atlantic City would be a perfect move for me, being that I had a degree in business and was an expert in marketing. Atlantic City was mostly famous for one thing: the casinos. I already figured out the best way to advertise and promote a casino. Tell the gamblers that they have a high chance of winning a large amount of money. It works every time! So it wouldn't be hard for me to snag a career in my field and get rich while doing so.

Something really important had recently come up, and my father was forced to miss my graduation ceremony. His only son was graduating and he couldn't even attend. It was all right because I was determined to make it on my own anyway. My father had many connections with some big executives in the casino industry. My father owned his own construction business, and it opened up many doors that are closed to an average person. My father wanted me to work for him and help promote his business, but I decided it was a bigger fish in the sea I was after: the place that never closes, the place where the opportunities are endless. My old man was a very understanding man and he respected my wishes. As a matter of fact, he would even help me get a job in one of the casinos. His company was doing really well for itself, so he figured the casino would be perfect for me.

Mark my college roommate nicknamed me "The Gambler" because I had taken chances that others wouldn't consider taking. I figure, if you don't take chances when an opportunity presents itself, then how do you know how far you can go in life. I was succeeding in life at a rapid speed, and I had to make some serious choices in life. I will take a gamble every now and then, and so far it's paid off. Mark and I did plenty to make it through these hard college years. For the past three years, Mark and I had become really close, like brothers. He was the reason I established a nicely sized bankroll, and if a roommate could help me do that, becoming close with him didn't take me long.

Mark and the rest of the juniors were finishing their final exams. He and a few buddies of ours were coming over for a last traditional poker game. Even though Mark was only a junior, he was very mature for his age. He was born in Los Angles, California. For some reason he said the east coast had more to offer him, so he decided to go to school at Boston University. Mark didn't get along with his old man and wanted to go to school as far away as possible, even if it he had to travel on the other side of the country.

I kept Mark around for a couple of reasons, but the main reason was because the boy was a pure genius. He was the reason I made the dean's list for three years straight. The kid had all types of ways of acing an exam. I remember sometime last year a classroom with about seventy-five students. Mark actually went inside the lab room and took my physics exam for me, without the professor ever finding out. Some of the stuff he pulled off was just unbelievable.

Mark was also the reason I kept money in my pocket on a regular basis; he was the master at the game we call poker, and he taught me everything I knew about it. He taught me when to bluff, when to fold, and most importantly when to bet.

Every Saturday night there was secret poker game on campus. Certain students knew exactly where the game would be held. We changed the location every week. We did this so the dean and his staff could not track us down, since gambling for money was illegal on campus. The pot got as high as five hundred dollars some games. My hustled was winning that poker's pot every week.

We had some great times at this college, and it was finally coming to an end. The females in this school were some of the prettiest girls in the country. It was nearly impossible to just date one. I don't know how I managed to choose one, but I did!

My dating problems came to end when I saw the most gorgeous girl I had ever seen in my life. Her name was

Gloria Williams, and she was also a junior. She was from upstate New York: Yonkers. Gloria was mixed; her father was a Black stockbroker who was very successful in the stock market trade, and her mother was this attractive white lady with the prettiest legs I had ever seen. I still can't believe that she was Gloria's mother. Gloria had one of her mother's pictures hanging on her wall. They looked liked they could be sisters.

Gloria had this honeycomb complexion with some green-hazel eyes. She had these small, pointy breasts with a Jennifer Lopez's ass. Her body was shaped like—how can I say—like one of those old Coca Cola bottles. She had a body that men only see in their dreams. She was just so fine! I wanted her in my life as soon as I laid eyes on her. I just knew that she was going to be mine. After running game to her for a whole semester, she finally agreed to go out with me. She was the sweetest and most innocent person I had ever met. I promised her that day I would marry her.

My cell phone rang and Gloria picture appeared in my cell phone. That's when I answered it.

"Hello."

"It's me, baby. I just finished my last exam and I'll be over there with in five minutes." She wanted me to do what I do best, and that was to please her every need. She wanted it one more time before I headed home. What can I say; she was addicted to it. The only thing was Mark was also finishing up his exams as well and should be here shorthly. I figured I had about twenty minutes before Mark and the rest of guys got here. Gloria would be here in five minutes. That give me about fifteen minutes. I jumped in the shower. Then I would take care of Gloria's needs and be able to set up the poker game for the fellows. That's when there was a silent knock at the door. Knock, knock.

The room was steaming hot from the shower running. I wanted to freshen up for her before she got here. It would save me the time of getting dressed and then getting undressed again. We could get right to it.

I got out of the shower and answered the door.

"Who is it?" I asked with one of my sexy man voices, praying it wasn't Mark. I opened the door and my prayers were answered. Gloria was standing there looking so sexy I immediately got aroused. The towel that was wrapped around my half-naked body grew about an extra nine inches. She took one glance at the large bulge and grinned.

"You must be happy to see me," Gloria said, staring directly at my crotch the whole time.

"Come on in, girl, before I catch a cold. So how did you do on those exams?" I asked her.

She shrugged her shoulders like that was last thing on her mind. That's when I knew actually what she wanted.

"Well we do have about fifteen minutes until Mark gets here and…"

And before I could say another word, she dropped her skirt and she was standing there in a G-string thong and those perky, tiny titties that I love so much. I grabbed her and threw her on the bed. She then turned herself around, slamming her face in the pillows and putting her rounded ass up in the air. That's when I pushed the G string to the side and put the whole nine inches in her. She moaned as my huge dick pounded her from behind. She loved every moment of it; she was a bigger freak than me in bed. I couldn't believe it. I was about to graduate and I had Gloria for a girlfriend. Life couldn't get any better.

Soon coming to AuthorHouse…